"How about if I confess something that is hard for me to admit?

I find you attractive."

"Why would you tell me something like that?"

"It gives you a little power over me," she said with a sexy, sweet smile that sent an electric pulse zipping along his nerve endings.

"And you think I need that," he countered, bothered that she had him all figured out. Well, maybe not all figured out. But she had a pretty good idea of what made him tick. It served as a reminder that he needed to stay on his guard around her.

"Don't you?" Her presumptive manner bordered on overconfidence. "I think you crave being in control at all times and I'll bet it drives you crazy when things don't go according to plan."

"I don't go crazy," he said, stepping into her space, unwilling to consider his real motivation for what he was about to do. "I adapt."

Lia misjudged the reason Paul closed the gap between them and never saw the kiss coming.

* ** *

Seductive Secrets is part of the
Sweet Tea and Scandal series.

Dear Reader,

I'm excited to bring you the fourth installment of my Sweet Tea and Scandal series set in Charleston. I've loved doing research on this historic town and creating scandalous stories to set there.

Plots where opposites attract are always fun to write, so I thought why not throw a suspicious cybersecurity specialist and a free-spirited wanderer together in a mad scheme and watch sparks fly. Toss in a case of mistaken identity and a couple of all-too-accurate tarot card readings and these two can't resist their secret attraction despite the danger it poses if the truth gets out.

I hope you enjoy Lia and Paul's story.

Happy reading!

Cat Schield

CAT SCHIELD

SEDUCTIVE SECRETS

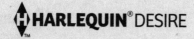

HARLEQUIN® DESIRE

Recycling programs
for this product may
not exist in your area.

ISBN-13: 978-1-335-60396-8

Seductive Secrets

www.Harlequin.com

Printed in U.S.A.

Cat Schield is an award-winning author of contemporary romances for Harlequin Desire. She likes her heroines spunky and her heroes swoonworthy. While her jet-setting characters live all over the globe, Cat makes her home in Minnesota with her daughter, two opinionated Burmese cats and a goofy Doberman. When she's not writing or walking dogs, she's searching for the perfect cocktail or traveling to visit friends and family. Contact her at www.catschield.com.

Books by Cat Schield

Harlequin Desire

Las Vegas Nights

The Black Sheep's Secret Child
Little Secret, Red Hot Scandal
The Heir Affair

Sweet Tea and Scandal

Upstairs Downstairs Baby
Substitute Seduction
Revenge with Benefits

Visit her Author Profile page at Harlequin.com, or catschield.com, for more titles!

You can find Cat Schield on Facebook, along with other Harlequin Desire authors, at Facebook.com/harlequindesireauthors!

One

Paul Watts entered the hospital elevator and jabbed the button for the fourth floor with more force than necessary. In two hours he was leaving Charleston to attend a week-long cybersecurity conference. His gut told him this was a mistake. His eighty-five-year-old grandfather's medical situation wasn't improving. Grady had been hospitalized six days earlier with cerebral edema, a complication arising from the massive stroke he'd suffered three months earlier that had affected his speech and left one side of his body paralyzed. In the midst of this latest medical crisis, the family worried that Grady wouldn't last much longer. Which was why Paul was rethinking his trip.

Despite the excellent care he was receiving from the doctors, the Watts family patriarch was failing to rally.

At first the doctors and physical therapists had agreed that the likelihood of Grady making a full recovery was better than average given his excellent health before the stroke and his impossibly strong will. But he hadn't mended. And he hadn't fought. The stroke had stolen more than his voice and muscle control. It had broken Grady Watts.

Although he'd stepped down as CEO of the family shipping empire a decade earlier and turned over the day-to-day running of the corporation to Paul's father, Grady had remained as chairman of the board. Not one to slow down, he'd kept busy in "retirement" by sitting on the boards of several organizations and maintained an active social life.

Accustomed to his grandfather's tireless vigor, stubbornness and unapologetic outspokenness, Paul couldn't understand why Grady wouldn't strive to get well, and thanks to the strained relationship between them, Paul was unlikely to get answers. Their estrangement was an ache that never went away. Still, Paul refused to regret his decision to pursue a career in cybersecurity rather than join the family business. Stopping bad guys satisfied his need for justice in a way that running the family shipping company never would.

The elevator doors opened and Paul stepped into the bright, sterile corridor that ran past the nurses' station. He offered brief nods to the caregivers behind the desk as he strode the far-too-familiar hallways that led to his grandfather's private room.

His steps slowed as he neared where Grady lay so still and beaten. No one would ever accuse Paul of being fainthearted, but he dreaded what he'd find when he entered the room. Every aspect of his life had been influenced by his grandfather's robust personality and Grady's current frailty caused Paul no small amount of dismay. Just as his grandfather had lost the will to go on, Paul's confidence had turned into desperation. He would do or support anything that would inspire Grady to fight his way back to them.

Reaching his grandfather's room, Paul gathered a deep breath. As he braced himself to enter, a thread of music drifted through the small gap between the door and frame. A woman was singing something sweet and uplifting. Paul didn't recognize the pure, clear voice and perfect pitch as belonging to anyone in his family. Perhaps it was one of the nurses. Had one of them discovered that his grandfather loved all kinds of music?

Paul pushed open the door and stepped into his grandfather's dimly lit room. The sight that greeted him stopped him dead in his tracks. Grady lay perfectly still, his skin gray and waxy. If not for the reassuring beep of the heart monitor, Paul might've guessed his grandfather had already passed.

On the far side of the bed, her back to the darkened window, a stranger held Grady's hand. Despite her fond and gentle expression, Paul went on instant alert. She wasn't the nurse he'd expected. In fact, she wasn't any sort of ordinary visitor. More like someone who'd wandered away from an amusement park. Or the sixth-floor psychiatric ward.

Pretty, slender and in her midtwenties, she wore some sort of costume composed of a lavender peasant dress and a blond wig fastened into a thick braid and adorned with fake flowers. Enormous hazel eyes dominated a narrow face with high cheekbones and a pointed chin. She looked like a doll come to life.

Paul was so startled that he forgot to moderate his voice. "Who are you?"

The question reverberated in the small space, causing the woman to break off midsong. Her eyes went wide and she froze like a deer caught in headlights. Her rosy lips parted on a startled breath and her chest rose on an inhalation, but Paul fired off another question before she answered the first.

"What are you doing in my grandfather's room?"

"I'm…" Her gaze darted past him toward the open door.

"Geez, Paul, calm the hell down," said a voice from behind him. It was his younger brother, Ethan. His softer tone suited the hospital room far better than Paul's sharp bluster. "I heard you all the way down the hall. You're going to upset Grady."

Now Paul noticed that his grandfather's eyes were open and his mouth was working as if he had an opinion he wanted to share. The stroke had left him unable to form the words that let him communicate, but there was no question Grady was agitated. His right hand fluttered. The woman's bright gaze flicked from Paul to Grady and back.

"Sorry, Grady." Paul advanced to his grandfather's bedside and lightly squeezed the old man's cool, dry fingers, noting the tremble in his knobby knuckles. "I came by to check on you. I was surprised to see this stranger in your room." He glanced toward the oddly dressed woman and spoke in a low growl. "I don't know who you are, but you shouldn't be here."

"Yes, she should." Ethan came to stand beside Paul, behaving as if introducing his brother to a woman dressed in costume was perfectly ordinary.

This lack of concern made Paul's blood pressure rise. "You know her?"

"Yes, this is Lia Marsh."

"Hello," she said, her bright sweet voice like tinkling crystal.

As soon as Ethan had entered the room her manner had begun to relax. Obviously she viewed Paul's brother as an ally. Now she offered Paul a winsome smile. If she thought her charm would blunt the keen edge of his suspicion, she had no idea who she was dealing with. Still, he found the anxiety that had plagued him in recent days easing. A confusing and unexpected sense of peace trickled through him as Grady's faded green eyes focused on Lia Marsh. He seemed happy to have her by his side, weird costume and all.

"I don't understand what she's doing here," Paul complained, grappling to comprehend this out-of-control situation.

"She came to cheer up our grandfather." Ethan set a comforting hand on their grandfather's shoulder. "It's okay," he told the older man. "I'll explain everything to Paul."

What was there to explain?

During the brothers' exchange, the woman squeezed Grady's hand. "I've really enjoyed our time together today," she said, her musical voice a soothing oasis in the tense room. "I'll come back and visit more with you later."

Grady made an unhappy noise, but she was already moving toward the foot of the bed. Paul ignored his grandfather's protest and shifted to intercept her.

"No, you won't," he declared.

"I understand," she said, but her expression reflected dismay and a trace of disapproval. Her gaze flicked to Ethan. A warm smile curved her lips. "I'll see you later."

Embroidered skirt swishing, she moved toward the exit, leaving a ribbon of floral perfume trailing in her wake. Paul caught himself breathing her in and expelled the tantalizing scent from his lungs in a vigorous huff. The energy in the room plummeted as she disappeared through the doorway and, to his profound dismay, Paul was struck by a disconcerting urge to call her back.

Now just to get answers to the most obvious questions: Why was she dressed like that and what was she doing in Grady's room? But also why had she chosen to tattoo a delicate lily of the valley on the inside of her left wrist? He wondered how his brother could be taken in by such guileless naivete when it was so obviously an act.

This last point snapped Paul out of whatever spell she'd cast over him. Grabbing his brother's arm, Paul towed Ethan out of the hospital room, eager to get answers without disturbing Grady. Out in the hall, Paul closed the door and glanced around. Lia Marsh had vanished and he noticed that didn't bring him the satisfaction it should have.

"Who is she?" Paul demanded, his unsettled emotions making his tone sharper than necessary. "And what the hell is going on?"

Ethan sighed. "Lia's a friend of mine."

Paul dragged his hand through his hair as he fought to control the emotions cascading through him. He focused on his anxiety over his grandfather's condition. That feeling made sense. The rest he would just ignore.

"You've never mentioned her before," Paul said. "How well do you know her?"

A muscle jumped in Ethan's jaw. He looked like he was grappling with something. "Well enough. Look, you're seeing problems where there aren't any."

"Have you forgotten that Watts Shipping as well as various members of our family have been cyberattacked in the last year? So when I show up in Grady's hospital room and there's a strange woman alone with him, I get concerned."

"Trust me—Lia has nothing to do with any of that," Ethan said. "She's really sweet and just wants to help. Grady has been so depressed. We thought a visit might cheer him up."

Paul refused to believe that he'd overreacted. And Ethan was transitioning into the CEO position at Watts Shipping, replacing their father who planned to retire in the next year. Why wouldn't his brother take these various cyber threats seriously?

"But she was dressed like a…like a…" It wasn't like

him to grapple for words, but the whole encounter had a surreal quality to it.

"Disney princess?" Ethan offered, one corner of his mouth kicking up. "Specifically Rapunzel from *Tangled*."

"Okay, but you never answered my question. Where did you meet her?" Paul persisted, making no attempt to rein in his skepticism. Ethan's persistent caginess was a red flag. "What do you know about her?"

When meeting people for the first time, Paul tended to assess them like it was an investigation and often struggled to give them the benefit of the doubt. Did that mean he was suspicious by nature? Probably. But if that's what it took to keep his family safe, then so be it.

"Can you stop thinking like a cop for two seconds?" Ethan complained.

Paul bristled. It wasn't only Grady who hadn't supported his decision to join the Charleston PD after college and several years later start his cybersecurity business.

"What's her angle?"

"She doesn't have one. She's exactly like she seems."

Paul snorted. A cosplay fanatic? "What else do you know about her?"

"I don't know," Ethan complained, growing impatient. "She's really nice and a great listener."

"A great listener," Paul echoed, guessing that Lia Marsh had taken advantage of Ethan's distress over their grandfather's illness. "I suppose you told her all about Grady and our family?"

"It's not as if any of it is a huge secret."

"Regardless. You brought a complete stranger, some-one you know almost nothing about, to meet our dying grandfather." Paul made no effort to temper his irrita-tion. "What were you thinking?"

"I was thinking Grady might enjoy a visit from a sweet, caring person who has a beautiful singing voice." Ethan gave him such a sad look. "Why do you always go to the worst-case scenario?"

Paul stared at his brother. Ethan behaved as if this explanation made all the sense in the world. Meanwhile, Paul's relentless, logical convictions prevented him from grasping what sort of eccentricities drove Lia Marsh to parade around as a storybook character.

"She was dressed up. I just don't understand…"

Ethan shrugged. "It's what she does."

"For a living?"

"Of course not," Ethan countered, showing no de-fensiveness at all in the face of his brother's sarcasm. In fact, he looked fairly smug as he said, "She dresses up and visits sick children. They love her."

Paul cursed. Actually, that was a damned nice thing to do.

"How did you meet her?"

Ethan frowned. "I'm a client."

"What sort of a client?"

"None of this matters." Ethan exhaled. "Lia is great and your trust issues are getting old."

A heavy silence fell between the brothers as Paul brushed aside the criticism and brooded over Ethan's caginess. He hated being at odds with his brother and wasn't sure how to fix the disconnect. With less than a year between them in age, he and Ethan had been tight as kids despite their differing interests and passions. Paul was fascinated by technology and could spend hours alone, turning electronic components into useful devices, while Ethan was more social and preferred sports over schoolwork.

Both had excelled through high school and into college. And while they'd never directly competed over anything, once Paul decided against joining the family business, a subtle tension started growing between the siblings.

"You might as well tell me what's going on because you know I'll investigate and find out exactly who Lia Marsh is."

Lia Marsh blew out a sharp breath as she cleared the hospital room and fled down the empty hallway, noting her thudding heart and clammy palms. While Ethan hadn't glossed over his brother's suspicious nature, she hadn't been prepared for Paul's hostility or the way his annoyance heightened his already imposing charisma. Unaccustomed to letting any man get under her skin, Lia studied the phenomenon like she would a fresh scratch on her beloved camper trailer, Misty. Unexpected and undesirable.

Usually her emotions were like dandelion fluff on the wind, lighter than air and streaked with sunshine. She embraced all the joy life had to offer and vanquished negativity through meditation, crystal work and aromatherapy, often employing these same spiritual healing tools with her massage clients. Not all of them bought into new age practices, but some surprised her with their interest. For instance, she never imagined a businessman like Ethan Watts opening his mind to ancient spiritual practices, but his curiosity demonstrated that it was never wise to prejudge people.

Someone should share that warning with Paul Watts. He'd obviously jumped to several conclusions from the instant he'd spotted her in his grandfather's hospital room. The unsettling encounter left her emotions swirling in a troubling combination of excitement and dread, brought on by a rush of physical attraction and her aversion to conflict.

Distracted by her inner turmoil, Lia found it impossible to sink back into her role of Rapunzel as she stole along the corridor lit by harsh fluorescent lights. Her gaze skimmed past gray walls and bland landscapes. Recycled air pressed against her skin, smelling of disinfectant. She longed to throw open a window and invite in sunshine and breezes laden with newly cut grass and bird song. Instead, she dressed up and visited sick children, offering a much-needed diversion.

Heading down the stairs to the third-floor pediatric wing, Lia collected her tote bag from the nurses' station. Since signing up to volunteer at the hospital these last few months, she'd been a frequent visitor and the children's care staff had grown accustomed to her appearances. They appreciated anything that boosted their patients' spirits and gave them a break from the endless rounds of tests or treatments.

The elevator doors opened and Lia stepped into the car. She barely noticed the mixed reactions of her fellow passengers to her outfit. Minutes later Lia emerged into the late afternoon sunshine. She sucked in a large breath and let it out, wishing she could shake her lingering preoccupation with her encounter with Paul Watts. Lia picked up her pace as if she could outrun her heightened emotions.

The traffic accident that had totaled her truck and damaged her beloved camper had compelled her to move into a one-bedroom rental on King Street until she could afford to replace her vehicle. Her temporary living arrangement was a twenty-minute walk from the hospital through Charleston's historic district. She focused on the pleasant ambience of the antebellum homes she passed, the glimpses of private gardens through wrought iron fencing, and savored the sunshine warming her shoulders.

Caught up in her thoughts, Lia barely noticed the man leaning against the SUV parked in front of her apartment until he pushed off and stepped into her path. Finding her way blocked, her pulse jumped. Lia had traveled the country alone since she was eighteen and had good instincts when it came to strangers. Only this was someone she'd already met.

Paul Watts had the sort of green eyes that reminded her of a tranquil pine forest, but the skepticism radiating from him warned Lia to be wary. Despite that, his nearness awakened the same buzz of chemistry that she'd noticed in the hospital room.

He wasn't at all her type. He was too obstinate. Too grounded. Merciless. Resolute. Maybe that was the attraction.

"You were hard to find," Paul declared.

Ethan had told her Paul was a former cop who now ran his own cybersecurity business. She suspected his single-minded focus had stopped a high number of cybercriminals. Her skin prickled at the idea that he'd do a deep dive into her background where things lurked that she'd prefer remained buried.

"And yet here you are," she retorted, dismayed that he'd run her down in the time it had taken her to walk home.

She wasn't used to being on anyone's radar. To most of her massage clients she was a pair of hands and a soothing voice. The kids at the hospital saw only their favorite princess character. She relished her anonymity.

"Is everything all right with Grady?"

"He's fine." Paul's lips tightened momentarily as a flash of pain crossed his granite features. "At least he isn't any worse."

"I didn't know him before his stroke, but Ethan said he was strong and resilient. He could still pull through."

"He could," Paul agreed, "except it's as if he's given up."

"Ethan mentioned he'd become obsessed with reuniting with his granddaughter these last few years," Lia said. "Maybe if you found her—"

"Look," Paul snapped. "I don't know what you're up to, but you need to stay away from my grandfather."

"I'm not up to anything," Lia insisted, pulling her key out of her bag as she angled toward the building's front door. "All I want to do is help."

"He doesn't need your help."

"Sure. Okay." At least he hadn't barred her from connecting with Ethan. "Is that it?"

She'd unlocked the door and pushed it open, intending to escape through it when Paul spoke again.

"Aren't you the least bit curious how I found you?" he asked, his vanity showing. Given her minimal electronic footprint, tracking her down left him puffed up with pride. No doubt he wanted to brag about his prowess.

Despite the agitation making her heart thump, Lia paused in the doorway and shot him a sidewise glance. While Paul exuded an overabundance of confidence and power, she wasn't without strengths of her own. She would just have to combat his relentlessness with freewheeling flirtation.

While teasing Paul was a danger similar to stepping too near a lion's cage, Lia discovered having his full attention was exhilarating.

"Actually." Pivoting to face him, Lia summoned her cheekiest smile. Everything she'd heard from Ethan indicated that Paul was ruled by logic rather than his emotions. Challenging the cybersecurity expert to confront his feelings was bound to blow up in her face. "I'm more intrigued that you wanted to."

Two

King Street melted away around him as Paul processed his response to Lia's challenging grin. Her expression wasn't sexual in nature, but that didn't lessen the surge of attraction that rocked him, demanding that he act. He clenched his hands behind his back to stifle the impulse to snatch her into his arms and send his lips stalking down her neck in search of that delectable fragrance. Frustrating. Intolerable. This woman was trouble. In more ways than he had time to count.

What was her endgame? Money, obviously.

Based on the fact that she'd chosen to live in one of downtown Charleston's priciest neighborhoods, she obviously had expensive taste. After meeting Ethan, she'd obviously targeted him, using their grandfather's illness to ingratiate herself. Was she planning on getting Ethan to pay off her debt or to invest in some sort of business?

"Ophelia Marsh, born March first—" he began, determined to unnerve her with a quick rundown of her vital statistics.

"Fun fact," she interrupted. "I was almost a leap-day baby. My mom went into labor late on February twenty-eighth and everyone thought for sure I would be born the next day, which that year was February twenty-ninth. But I didn't want to have a birthday every four years. I mean, who would, right?"

Her rambling speech, sparkling with energetic good humor, soured his mood even more. "Right." He had no idea why he was agreeing. "Born March first in Occidental, California…"

"A Pisces."

He shook his head. "A what?"

"A Pisces," she repeated. "You know, the astrological sign. Two fish swimming in opposite directions. Like you're a goat," she concluded.

Paul exhaled harshly. Horoscopes were nothing but a bunch of nonsense. Yet that didn't stop him from asking, "I'm a goat?"

"A Capricorn. You just had a birthday."

He felt her words like a hit to his solar plexus. "How did you know that?"

Her knowing his birthday filled him with equal parts annoyance and dismay. *He* was the security expert, the brilliant investigator who hunted down cybercriminals and kept his clients' data safe. To have this stranger know something as personal as his birth date sent alarm jolting through him.

"Ethan told me."

"Why would he do that?" Paul demanded, directing the question to the universe rather than Lia.

"Why wouldn't he?" She cocked her head and regarded him as if that was obvious. "He likes to talk about his family and it helps me to picture all of you if I know your signs. You're a Capricorn. Your mother is a Libra. She's the peacekeeper of the family. Your father is a Sagittarius. He's a talker and tends to chase impossible dreams. Ethan is a Taurus. Stubborn, reliable, with a sensual side that loves good food."

This quick summary of his family was so spot-on that Paul's suspicions reached even higher levels. Obviously, this woman had been researching the Wattses for some nefarious purpose. What was she up to? Time to turn up the volume on his questioning.

"You don't stay in one place for very long," he said, remembering what he'd managed to dig up on her. "New York, Vermont, Massachusetts, now South Carolina, all visited in the last twelve months. Why is that?"

In his experience grifters liked to work an area and move on when things became too hot. Her pattern fit with someone up to no good. She might be beautiful and seem to possess a sweet, generous nature, but in his mind her obvious appeal worked against her. He knew firsthand how easily people were taken in by appearances. He was more interested in substance.

"I'm a nomad."

"What does that mean?"

"It means I like life on the road. It's how I grew up." She paused to assess his expression and whatever she glimpsed there made her smile slightly. "I was born in the back of a VW camper van and traveled nearly five thousand miles in the first year of my life. My mother has a hard time staying put for any long period of time."

Paul was having a difficult time wrapping his head around what she was saying. For someone who belonged to a family that had lived within ten square miles of Charleston for generations, he couldn't fathom the sort of lifestyle she was talking about.

"Was your mother on the run from someone? Your father? Or a boyfriend?"

"No." Her casual shrug left plenty of room for Paul to speculate. "She was just restless."

"And you? Are you restless, too?"

"I guess." Something passed over her features, but it was gone too fast for him to read. "Although I tend to stay longer in places than she did."

Follow-up questions sprang to Paul's mind, but he wasn't here to dig into her family dynamic. He needed to figure out what she was up to so he could determine how much danger she represented to his family. He changed subjects. "Where did you and Ethan meet?"

"He's been a client of mine for about a month now."

"A client?" Paul digested this piece of information.

"I work for Springside Wellness," she said, confirming what Paul had already unearthed about her. The company was a wellness spa on Meeting Street that operated as both a yoga studio and alternative treatment space. A lot of mind, body, soul nonsense. "Ethan is a client."

This confirmed what Paul had gleaned from his brother's explanation about how he knew Lia. Still, Paul had a hard time picturing his brother doing yoga and reflexology. "What sort of a client?"

"I'm a massage therapist. He comes in once a week. I told him he should probably come in more often than that. The man is stressed."

Her answer took Paul's thoughts down an unexpected path. "Well, that's just perfect."

Only it wasn't perfect at all. A picture of Lia giving Ethan a massage leaped to mind but he immediately suppressed it.

"I don't understand what you mean," she said, frowning. "And I don't have time to find out. I have to be at work in an hour and it takes a while for me to get out of costume. Nice to meet you, Paul Watts."

He quite pointedly didn't echo the sentiment. "Just remember what I said about staying away from my grandfather."

"I already said I would."

With a graceful flutter of her fingers, she zipped through the building's front door, leaving him alone on the sidewalk. Despite her ready agreement to keep her distance, his nerves continued to sizzle and pop. Logic told him he'd seen the last of Lia Marsh, but his instincts weren't convinced.

Paul shot his brother a text before sliding behind the wheel, urging him to reiterate to Lia that Grady was off-limits. Thanks to this detour he was going to have to hustle to keep from being late for his charter flight.

Ethan's terse reply highlighted the tension between the brothers that seemed to be escalating. The growing distance between them frustrated Paul, but he couldn't figure out how to fix what he couldn't wrap his head around.

Pushing Ethan and the problem of Lia Marsh to the back of his mind, Paul focused his attention on something concrete and within his control: the upcoming conference and what he hoped to get out of it.

As much as Ethan had thoroughly enjoyed seeing his brother utterly flummoxed by Lia in a Rapunzel costume, as soon as Paul headed off to dig into her background, Ethan's satisfaction faded. Leave it to his brother to chase a tangent rather than deal with the real problem of their grandfather's condition. In the same way, Ethan's brother had neatly avoided dealing with Grady's disappointment after Paul chose a career in law enforcement over joining Watts Shipping and eventually taking his place at the helm of the family business. Nor had Paul understood Ethan's conflicted emotions at being the second choice to take up the reins.

While Ethan recognized that he was the best brother to head the family company, he wanted to secure the job based on his skills, not because Paul refused the position. Also, it wasn't just his pride at issue. Ethan was adopted and in a city as preoccupied with lineage as Charleston, not knowing who his people were became a toxic substance eating away at his peace of mind.

Although no one had ever made him feel as if he didn't belong, in every Watts family photo, Ethan's dark brown hair and eyes made him stand out like a goose among swans. Not wishing to cause any of his family undue pain, he kept his feelings buried, but more and more lately they'd bubbled up and tainted his relationship with Paul.

He'd shared some of his angst with Lia. She was a good listener. Attentive. Nonjudgmental. Empathetic. Sure, she was a little quirky. But Ethan found her eccentricities charming. That Paul viewed them as suspect made Ethan all the more determined to defend her.

Clamping down on his disquiet, Ethan reentered his grandfather's hospital room and noted that Grady's eyes were open and sharp with dismay. Had he heard the brothers arguing in the hallway? Although Grady never shied away from confrontation, before the stroke, he'd confided to Ethan that he was troubled by his estrangement from Paul and also the growing tension between the brothers. Ethan knew Paul was equally frustrated with the rift, but none of them had taken any steps to overcome the years of distance.

"Sorry about earlier," Ethan murmured, settling into the chair between Grady's bed and the window. "You know how Paul can get."

He didn't expect Grady to answer. In the weeks following the stroke, Grady had made some progress with the paralysis. He still couldn't walk or write, but he'd regained the ability to move his arm, leg and fingers. It wasn't so much his body that had failed him, but his willingness to fight.

Grady's lips worked, but he couldn't form the words for what he wanted to express. For the first time in weeks this seemed to frustrate him.

"He worries about you," Ethan continued. "Seeing Lia here was a bit of a shock." He couldn't suppress a grin. "Did you like her Rapunzel costume? The kids down on the pediatric floor really loved her."

Grady started to hum a toneless tune Ethan didn't recognize. And then all at once he sang a word.

"Ava."

Ethan was shocked that Grady had spoken—or rather sung—his daughter's name. "You mean Lia," he said, wondering how his grandfather could've confused his daughter for Lia. Blonde and green-eyed Ava Watts bore no resemblance to Lia, with her dark hair and hazel eyes. Then Ethan frowned. Had Lia ever come to visit as herself or was she always in costume? Maybe Grady thought she was blonde. And then there was the age difference. If Ava had lived, she'd be in her forties. Of course, the stroke had messed with the left side of Grady's brain where logic and reason held court. Maybe he was actually mixed up.

Ava had been eighteen when she'd run away to New York City. The family had lost track of her shortly thereafter. And it wasn't until five years after that that they found out she'd died, leaving behind an infant daughter. The child had been adopted, but they'd never been able to discover anything more because the files had been sealed.

"Ava…baby," Grady clarified, singing the two words. How had he learned to do that?

"You think Lia is Ava's daughter?" While Grady nodded as enthusiastically as his condition allowed, Ethan's stunned brain slowly wrapped itself around this development. Grady was obviously grasping at thin air. With each year that passed he'd grown more obsessed with finding his missing granddaughter.

"Ava's daughter is here?" Constance Watts asked from the doorway. "Where? How?"

Ethan turned to his mother, about to explain what was going on, when his grandfather's fingers bit down hard on Ethan's wrist, drawing his attention back to the man in the bed. Grady's gaze bore the fierce determination of old, sending joy flooding through Ethan. What he wouldn't give to have his grandfather healthy and happy again.

"Ethan?" his mother prompted, coming to stand beside him.

"Lia..." Grady sang again, more agitated now as he tried to make himself understood.

"Lia?" Constance stared at her father-in-law, and then glanced at her son for clarification. "Who is Lia?"

But when the answer came, it was Grady who spoke up. "Ava...baby."

After her run-in with Paul Watts the day before, the last place Lia expected to find herself was seated beside Ethan in his bright blue Mercedes roadster on the way to the hospital to visit his grandfather. Overhead, clouds dappled the dazzling February sky. Around them the sweet scent of honeysuckle and crab apple blossoms mingled with the sound of church bells coming from the Cathedral of Saint Luke and Saint Paul. It was a glorious day for driving with the top down, but this was no joyride.

"I'm really not sure this is the best idea," Lia said, shuddering as she pictured her last encounter with Paul Watts. "Your brother was pretty clear that he didn't want me anywhere near your grandfather."

"Paul's occupation makes him suspicious," Ethan said. "And Grady's illness has made him even more edgy. Add to that the fact that he doesn't like surprises and that explains why he overreacted at finding a stranger visiting his grandfather." Ethan shot her a wry grin packed with boyish charm. "And you were dressed like Rapunzel so that had to throw him off, as well."

Lia rolled her eyes, unmoved by his attempt to lull her into giving up her argument. "Are you sure Paul will be okay with me visiting?"

She craved Ethan's reassurance. No one had ever treated her with the level of suspicion Paul Watts had shown.

"He wants Grady to get better just like the rest of us."

"That's not the same thing as being okay with my visiting," she pointed out, the churning in her stomach made worse by Ethan's evasion. Paul's bad opinion of her bothered Lia more than she liked to admit.

"Look, Paul's not in town at the moment so you don't need to worry about running into him. You just visit Grady a few more times and be the ray of sunshine that will enable him to improve and by the time Paul gets back, Grady will be on the mend and Paul will realize it was all due to you."

"I think you're overestimating my abilities," she demurred, even as Ethan's praise warmed her. Each time she'd visited Grady she held his hand and sung to him, pouring healing energy into his frail body.

"Trust me," Ethan declared, taking his espresso-colored eyes off the road and shooting a brief glance her way. "I'm not overestimating anything. Your visits have been transformative."

"But I've only been to see him four times," Lia murmured, determined to voice caution. If Ethan gave her all the credit for his grandfather's improvement, what happened if Grady took a turn for the worse? "I can't imagine I made that much of an impact."

"You underestimate yourself." Ethan spun the wheel and coasted into an empty spot in the parking garage. "He started communicating a little yesterday by singing the way you suggested. That's given him a huge boost in his outlook and he's growing better by the hour. You'll see."

In fact, Lia was excited to see Grady improve. She believed in the power of spiritual healing and trusted that she could tap into the energy that connected all living things and bring about change because she willed it. It didn't always work. Some concrete problems required real-world solutions. For instance, the broken axle on her camper trailer and her totaled truck.

Meditating hadn't gotten Misty fixed. She'd needed money and a mechanic for that. But after asking for help, the universe had found her a wonderful job, terrific coworkers and an affordable place to live. She'd been offered a solution at a point when she was feeling desperate.

Ethan shut off the engine and hit her with an eager grin. "Ready?"

"Sure." But in fact, she was anything but.

When they got off the elevator on the fourth floor, Ethan's long strides ate up the distance to his grandfather's hospital room, forcing Lia to trot in order to keep up.

As they neared Grady's room, Lia spied a familiar figure emerging. "Hi, Abigail," Lia said, as the distance between them lessened. "How is Grady doing today?"

For a moment the nurse looked startled that a stranger had called her by her name, but then she took a longer look at Lia and her eyes widened. "Lia! I didn't recognize you out of costume."

Lia gave an awkward chuckle and glanced at Ethan. "I'm not sure Grady will recognize me, either."

"Mr. Grady will know who you are." The nurse's reassuring smile did little to ease Lia's nerves. "There's a keen mind locked up in there." She glanced at Ethan and when he gave her a confirming nod, Abigail continued, "He's going to be so glad you've come today. Your idea to encourage him to sing has worked wonders. He's so excited to be able to communicate with people again."

Beside her, Ethan radiated smug satisfaction.

"That's great," Lia said, delighted that her suggestion had produced a positive result.

"His family and all the staff are so thrilled that things started to turn around yesterday. He's doing so much better that the doctor thinks he'll be able to go in a few days."

"Wow," Lia murmured, "that's wonderful news."

"We're so glad she showed up when she did," Ethan declared. "She's worked a miracle."

"Please stop," Lia protested, the praise making her uncomfortable. "The credit really should go to all of you who've been taking such good care of him this whole time."

"There's only so much medicine can do when the will to keep on living is gone," the nurse said.

"Mind over matter," Ethan said. "People don't give it enough credit."

"They certainly don't," Abigail agreed before heading down the hall toward the nurses' station.

Ethan set his hand on Lia's elbow and drew her into Grady's hospital room. As soon as she stepped across the threshold, Lia was struck by the room's buoyant energy. The first time she'd visited Grady Watts, he'd been an immobile lump beneath the covers, unconscious and unaware that she'd taken his hand and softly sung to him. Today as she stepped closer to the bed, she noticed that he was wide awake and eagerly watching her approach. The directness of his gaze reminded her of Paul and she shivered. Ethan had mentioned his grandfather had a sharp temper and forceful manner when crossed.

Grady wiggled his fingers and she took his hand. His dry skin stretched over bones knobby with arthritis. She gave his fingers a light squeeze, shocked at the rush of affection for someone she barely knew. Yet was that true?

Usually she moved on every couple months and rarely got tangled up in people's lives. In this case, her accident extended her time in Charleston, leading to numerous massage sessions with Ethan where he'd spoken at length about his family. As the weeks turned into months, Lia had grown ever more invested in their stories until she almost felt like part of their circle.

"Hello, Grady," Lia said, her voice warbling as affection tightened her throat. "It's Lia. You probably didn't recognize me without my costume. How are you feeling today? You look really good."

Grady's fingers pulsed against hers as he acknowledged her with two sung words. "Ava daughter."

Ethan had explained how Grady had been desperate to reunite with his missing granddaughter before the stroke, even speculating that the patriarch's illness had been brought on by the crushing disappointment of a recent dead end. Since then, Grady had brooded nonstop about what had become of her and the family's failure to bring her back into the fold.

"That's right, Grady," Ethan said, beaming at Lia. His eyes held a wicked twinkle as he added, "Ava's daughter has come home at last."

Delighted by the news, Lia glanced at Ethan and noticed the way the handsome businessman was regarding her with purposeful intent. Her heart began hammering against her ribs as the import of what Ethan was saying struck her. She shifted her attention to the man lying in the hospital bed and she caught her breath to protest. But before she could voice her sharp denial, she saw the love shining in Grady's eyes for her. No. Not for her. For his missing granddaughter.

Head spinning, Lia turned her full attention on Ethan. "What's going on?"

"What's going on is that Grady knows you're his granddaughter." Ethan gripped Lia's elbow with long fingers while his eyes beseeched her to go along. "I explained how Paul located you through one of those genetic testing companies. It's long been Grady's dream to reunite you with your family. And now here you are."

Lia's mind reeled. The position Ethan had put her in was untenable, and to drag his brother into the mix was only going to create more drama. But the sheer joy in Grady's eyes tied her tongue in knots. This could not be happening. She had to tell the truth. She wasn't Ava Watts's long-lost daughter. To claim that she was the missing Watts granddaughter would only lead to trouble.

"We need to talk about this," Lia growled quietly at Ethan. She put her hand on Grady's shoulder. "We'll be right back."

Leaving a confused Grady behind, Lia fled out into the hallway. To her relief, Ethan followed her. Worried that Grady might overhear their conversation, Lia grabbed Ethan's arm and towed him down the hall toward the waiting area near the bank of elevators.

"Have you lost your mind?" she whispered as soon as they reached the empty family lounge. "How could you tell him I'm his granddaughter? And why put Paul in the middle of it? He's going to be furious."

"Grady came to that conclusion all by himself," Ethan explained. "And the reason I gave Paul credit was to help repair the strained relationship between him and Grady."

"Your brother will never go along with this."

"He will when he sees the way Grady is recovering. Overnight his whole prognosis has changed. And it's all because he believes you're his granddaughter. It was his deepest desire to reunite with her and now he has a reason to live."

"But I'm not his granddaughter. Why would he think I am? I don't look like any of your family." Lia's heart twisted as she realized her protest might rouse Ethan's angst over being adopted.

"You could be Ava's daughter." Ethan lifted his hands in a beseeching gesture. "We've been trying for years to find her with no luck. I told you that after my aunt died, her baby was adopted and the records were sealed. Believing you're her has given Grady a reason to go on. Do you seriously want to go back in there and break his heart? He's been so depressed since the stroke. In less than a week you've brought him back from the brink of death."

Lia closed her eyes and spent several seconds listening to the pounding of her heart. This could not be happening. And yet it was.

"I just can't do this."

Besides being wrong, even if she agreed to a temporary stint as Grady Watts's missing granddaughter, there was no way Paul was going to let her take on the role.

"You can," Ethan insisted. "Making people feel better is what you do."

"Sure, but not like this," Lia protested. "And I don't want to lie to your family."

"I understand, but they aren't any good at keeping secrets. We've never thrown a successful surprise party or gotten into trouble without everyone in the family knowing about it. For this to work we need to leave them in the dark or else risk that someone will slip up and give you away."

From Ethan's aggrieved tone, this obviously bugged him, and Lia sympathized. Having been isolated from relatives all her life, she couldn't imagine having so many people in her business. Yet there was a flip side. Ethan could also count on his family to have his back.

"And what about Paul?" she quizzed. "Surely he's already dug up enough info on me to know I'm not your cousin."

"Let me handle my brother."

Lia slid sweaty palms along her jean-clad thighs. "Damn it, Ethan. You can't deceive your grandfather this way."

"I can if it means keeping Grady alive," Ethan said and his voice held genuine pain.

"It's a lie," Lia insisted, but she could feel her determination failing beneath the weight of Ethan's enthusiasm. "A big fat dangerous lie. And you know I wasn't planning on sticking around Charleston much longer. Misty is fixed. I almost have enough saved to replace my truck." While this was true, Lia didn't have enough to buy a quality vehicle she could trust. "It's time I got back on the road."

"All you need to do is stay a couple weeks until Grady's completely out of the woods and then we can reveal that a huge mistake was made with the genetic testing service." Something in Lia's expression must have betrayed her weakening resistance because Ethan nodded as if she'd voiced her agreement. "I've thought the whole thing through and I know this will work."

If she hadn't grown fond of the handsome Charleston businessman since he'd become her massage client six months earlier, she never would've agreed to hear him out, much less consider such a wild scheme, but the pain Ethan felt over his grandfather's illness had touched her heart. Plus, he'd made the whole scheme sound so reasonable. A couple of weeks of playacting and then she'd be on her way again. A bubble of hysteria rose inside her. What were more lies on top of the ones she was already telling?

"But I'll be lying not just to Grady, but your whole family. It's a cruel thing to do to all of them."

"I've thought about that, too, but if we do this right, they'll be so happy that Grady is healthy again that it will make the eventual disappointment of you not being family easier to bear." Ethan gripped her hands and hit her with a mega dose of confident charm.

Lia was rallying one last refusal when the elevator doors opened and a slender woman in an elegant suit the color of pistachios stepped off. Instead of immediately heading for the hallway that led to the hospital rooms, she glanced toward the family lounge. Her expression brightened when she spied them.

"Ethan," she said, coming toward them. "Glad to see you here."

"Hello, Mother." Ethan dipped his head and kissed her cheek. "This is Lia."

Constance Watts was every inch a genteel matriarch of the South with her blond hair styled in a long bob and her triple strand of pearls. Her keen blue eyes assessed the jeans and thrift-store T-shirt Lia wore and she braced herself for censure, but Constance only smiled warmly.

"Ethan told me all about you," Constance said, her captivating Southern drawl knotted with emotion.

"He did?" Lia hadn't yet agreed to the scheme and bristled at Ethan's presumption.

"Of course." Constance glanced from Lia to her son. "He said Paul found you through a genetic testing service."

"I'm really—" Lia began.

"Overwhelmed," Ethan broke in, closing his fingers around her hand and squeezing gently. He snared her gaze, his eyes reflecting both determination and apology. "And can you blame her? Finally connecting with her real family after all these years is pretty momentous."

Ethan's need and his mother's elation were a patch of quicksand, trapping Lia. To her dismay, she began nodding.

"Ava's daughter is finally home," Constance murmured, stepping forward and embracing Lia. "You are going to make Grady so happy."

Three

Paul was crossing the hotel lobby on his way to the first panel of the day when his phone buzzed. Incensed at Ethan for bringing a stranger into their grandfather's hospital room, Paul had been ignoring his brother's calls since leaving for the conference. He pulled out his phone and was on the verge of sending the call to voice mail when he spied his mother's picture on the screen. His first reaction was dread. Had Grady's health taken a turn for the worse? Is that why she was calling rather than checking in by text?

"What's wrong?" he demanded, shifting his trajectory toward a quiet nook opposite the reception desk. "Is Grady okay?"

"He's fine. In fact, he's doing better than ever." Constance Watts sounded breathless with delight. "I just wanted to update you that Grady is coming home from the hospital today."

"That's great news," Paul said, stunned by the up-swing in Grady's progress. "So he's finally rallying?"

"Thanks to Lia."

"Lia?" Hearing that woman's name was like touching a live wire. The jolt made his heart stop. "I don't under-stand." Paul believed in cold hard facts not instinct, but at the moment his gut was telling him something bad was happening. "How is she responsible for Grady's improved health?"

"I can't believe you'd have to ask," Paul's mother said. "Ethan told me you found her."

"He did?" Paul responded cautiously. Obviously, his brother had neglected to mention Paul's suspicions about the woman. "Has she been visiting Grady?"

Constance laughed. "She's been by his side constantly for days. Having her there has made his recovery noth-ing short of miraculous. All the hospital staff are talking about it."

"Grady's getting better?" The volume of Paul's re-lief almost drowned out the other tidbit his mother had dropped. Lia was visiting Grady despite being told to stay away.

Obviously Paul had underestimated just how intent she was on interfering with his family. Well, he'd send her packing as soon as he returned home.

"...Ava's daughter back in the fold."

Who was back? His mother had continued to prattle on while Paul had been preoccupied. He shook his head to reorient his thoughts.

"I'm sorry, Mother, it's really loud where I am. Can you repeat what you said?"

"I said, Grady is thrilled that you found Ava's daughter," Constance said.

"I found…" Now Paul understood why Ethan had been working so hard to get in touch.

"When are you coming home? Grady's been asking to see you."

For the first time in his adult life, Paul Watts had no words. While his mother waited for his reply, Paul's brain worked feverishly to unravel what could possibly be going on back in Charleston. What sort of crazy stunt was his brother trying to pull? And why? Lia had no more Watts blood than Eth…

Paul shut down the rest of that thought. He and Ethan might not share a biological bond, but they were brothers and Ethan was just as much a Watts as any of them. The same could not be said for a drifter like Lia Marsh.

He hadn't been idle over the last few days of the conference. He'd taken the time to dig into her background and what he'd come up with only reinforced his suspicion that she was some sort of con artist.

"Mother, I need to go." Paul hated to be rude, but he needed to talk to his brother immediately. "Can I call you later?"

"Of course. When are you coming home?"

He was scheduled to return home in three days' time. "I'm going to cut my trip short and catch a flight today."

"That's wonderful."

Paul hung up with his mother and immediately called Ethan. He wasn't surprised when it rolled over to voice mail. Snarling, Paul disconnected without delivering the scathing smackdown his brother so richly deserved. He sent his personal assistant a text about his change of plans so she could organize a flight for him, and then he headed to his suite to pack.

An hour later he was on his way to the airport. A second call to Ethan went unanswered, but this time Paul left an icy message, demanding to know what was going on. The hours between liftoff and touchdown gave Paul plenty of time to check in with the rest of his family and get a feel for what had been going on in his absence.

The situation had progressed further than he'd anticipated. What really burned him was how happy and unquestioning everyone was with the arrival of a stranger claiming to be Ava's daughter. Lia had charmed his parents, aunt and uncle as well as his three Shaw cousins. Nor would any of them listen when he pointed out that they didn't know anything about this woman who'd abruptly appeared in their midst. All they cared about was that Ava's daughter had come home and Grady had magically become healthy.

Eager to get the whole messy situation sorted out, once he arrived in Charleston Paul headed straight from the airport to Grady's estate. He parked on the wide driveway at the back of the property, noting that Ethan's car was absent. The heated lecture Paul wanted to deliver would have to wait.

Paul's breath came in agitated bursts as he wound his way along the garden path and approached the back of the house where a set of double stairs ascended to a broad terrace. Taking the steps two at a time, Paul crossed the terrace to the glass door that led into the kitchen. The room had been remodeled a few years ago to include a massive granite island, abundant cabinets, professional appliances and an updated surround for the fireplace. Two doorways offered access to the interior of the home. Paul chose the one that led into the broad entry hall. Immediately to his left, a set of stairs led upward. Paul's tension rose as he ascended.

The home had been designed with spacious rooms off a wide main hallway. Upstairs, the broad space between the bedrooms was utilized as a cozy lounge area for watching television from the comfortable couch or reading in one of the armchairs that overlooked the rear of the property—as his grandfather's nurse Rosie was doing at the moment. Although Paul recognized that his grandfather didn't require her hovering over him at all hours of the day and night, seeing her whiling her time away over a cup of tea and a novel disturbed him.

"How's he doing?"

Rosie looked up from her book and shot him a wry grin. "Go see for yourself."

Paul approached his grandfather's bedroom, bracing himself for the same dimly lit, hushed space it had become since Grady's stroke. But the scene he stepped into was the utter opposite. Stuttering to a halt just inside the door, Paul gaped in confusion and alarm. What the hell was going on here?

Someone had pulled the curtains back from the windows allowing light to fill the large space. Elvis Presley's "All Shook Up" poured from a speaker on the nightstand, almost drowning out the soothing trickle of water from a small fountain situated on the dresser. The scent of rosemary and lavender drifted toward Paul. As the aroma hit his senses, he noticed a slight boost to his energy and felt a whole lot calmer than he'd been in months. He shook off the sensations and scowled at the source of all his internal commotion.

Paul realized it was Lia who'd transformed Grady's master suite from dark and bleak to bright and festive. And it did seem to be having a magical effect. For the first time since his stroke, Paul's grandfather was sitting upright in bed, propped against an abundance of pillows, his bright gaze fixed on the woman standing beside him. Lia was chattering away while her hands stroked up and down Grady's arm, working the muscles.

A bewildering swirl of emotions cascaded through him at the sight of his grandfather looking so happy and…healthy. Gladness. Relief. Annoyance. This last was due to Lia. She looked so utterly normal without all the theatrical makeup and princess clothing. Today she wore a plain gray T-shirt and black yoga leggings that showed off her lean hips and thighs. A silky ponytail of brown hair swept forward to cascade over one delicate collarbone, while long bangs framed her narrow face with its pixie chin and bright red lips. Silver hoop earrings swung against her delicate jawline.

Paul's immediate impulse was to haul her out of the room and away from his grandfather. He didn't trust her despite finding nothing concrete in her background to support the warning in his gut. Just because she hadn't been caught didn't mean she wasn't up to no good. Nor did it help her case how swiftly she'd charmed his entire family into embracing her as one of their own.

Even as he fumed in frustration, Paul became aware of something hot and disturbing lying beneath his irritation. It was as if his anger had awakened an insistent, instinctive pulse of raw hunger. He cursed the untimely appearance of this single-minded lust for Lia Marsh. Being distracted by physical cravings was the last thing he needed.

As if alerted by his conflicting desires, Lia glanced his way. Within their frame of sooty lashes, her eyes locked on his. Pleasure roared through him as she bit down on her lower lip. Color flooded her cheeks and for a second he pondered what might happen if his awareness was reciprocated.

Paul ruthlessly swept such musing aside. What did it matter if she was attracted to him? But then he dialed back his annoyance. Could he use it to his advantage?

His thoughts must've shown on his face because a wary frown drew Lia's eyebrows together. Irritated that he'd given himself away, Paul scowled in return. With a grimace she shifted her attention to Grady. Her smile brightened with what appeared to be genuine affection. Paul's gut clenched as he took in the tableau.

"Look who's here," she murmured, indicating Paul.

His grandfather turned his head and the warmth in his welcoming smile filled Paul with blinding joy. It was as if all the years of estrangement had been never been.

"Paul."

At hearing his name spoken so clearly by his grandfather, a lump formed in Paul's throat and stuck there. Because the stroke had affected Grady's speech, he'd struggled to make himself understood these last few months. Obviously, the reports of Grady's improvement hadn't been exaggerated. But to credit this interloper was going too far. Lost in his circling thoughts, Paul still hovered where he'd stopped just inside the room until his grandfather tapped out some rhythms on a small drum next to him on the bed.

"That means come," Lia explained.

Completely bewildered by what was happening, Paul crossed to his grandfather's side and gave his arm a squeeze. "How are you feeling today?"

The routine question was completely unnecessary. This man bore no resemblance to the invalid from a week ago. At that point, with Grady growing weaker by the day, Paul would've moved heaven and earth to see the return of a mischievous glint to his grandfather's green eyes, which had so recently been dull with defeat and grief. What he glimpsed in Grady's manner was the exact change he'd longed for. But at what cost?

"Happy." A distinct pattern of tapping accompanied Grady's singing. While his voice was breathy and tuneless, the word came out surprisingly clear. Yet despite his joy, Paul was disturbed by how his grandfather's gaze settled fondly on the young woman massaging his hand. "Lia home."

"What's with the drum?" Paul asked Lia, grappling with his shock at Grady's rapid improvement and his attachment to the stranger who had invaded all their lives. Discomfort formed a hard knot in his chest. Although thrilled by his grandfather's improvement, Paul could see nothing but trouble barreling down the road toward them and cursed his brother for doing something so radical and foolish.

"I did some research on stroke recovery and discovered that music and rhythm can help lift a patient's spirits, enable them to communicate and improve their speech." Lia smiled fondly at Grady. "Tomorrow we're going to learn breathing rhythms and also practice meditating to music."

"What's all that supposed to do?"

"The medical explanation didn't make all that much sense to me," Lia said. "But there was something about how the brain processes information and how music can affect that in a positive way. I think that's why Grady can't speak, but he can sing."

Paul's chest tightened as hope surged and he set his jaw against a blast of raw emotion. From the way his grandfather beamed at Lia, it was obvious what everyone had been saying. Grady's improvement had been inspired by the return of his long-lost granddaughter. Only Lia wasn't Ava's daughter and Paul hated the fraud she and his brother were perpetrating.

So, what was he going to do? Paul had never lied to his grandfather. Many times in the past when he was a kid growing up, he'd done something wrong and no matter how bad the punishment, he'd always told Grady the truth. It was a point of pride to Paul that his grandfather trusted him without question.

If he continued to let Grady believe his granddaughter had returned to her family, what sort of damage was he doing to his relationship with his grandfather? Yet Grady's will to live seemed to have been restored by Lia's arrival. Could Paul figure out a way to get rid of her without causing his grandfather harm?

"Do you have a couple minutes to talk?" he asked as she finished massaging Grady's arm and carefully placed it back on the bed.

"Grady has a session with his physical therapist in ten minutes."

With the number of relatives coming and going these days, Paul didn't want his conversation with Lia interrupted or overheard. "I'll meet you by the pool."

On the flight back to Charleston, he'd prepared a number of ways to extricate her from his family. Now, with Grady's improvement hanging on her continued presence, he wasn't convinced sending her away was the best idea.

While he waited for Lia to arrive, Paul paced the concrete deck, oblivious to the tranquility offered by the turquoise rectangle of water, the lush landscaping and the peaceful twittering of the birds.

This whole situation would be more cut-and-dried if anything suspicious had appeared in her background check. But Paul had nothing concrete to prove that she might not be as transparent as she appeared. While deep in his gut he was certain that she was keeping secrets, Paul was a man who acted on facts not feelings.

When Lia arrived, Paul wasted no time making his position clear. "When I told you to stay away from my grandfather, I had no idea things would get this out of control. I don't know what you and my brother were thinking, but this can't go on."

Because his entire family had embraced her, it fell to Paul to remain detached and keep his guard up. That would be easier if she didn't stir his body and incite his emotions. And if she hadn't worked miracles with his grandfather.

"You're right," she agreed. "I shouldn't have let Ethan talk me into lying to everyone. I'm sorry. It's just Ethan was so desperate to help your grandfather. And believing that I'm his granddaughter has made him better."

Paul watched her expression, determined to see past her guileless facade to the truth. "You've done a good job making sure everyone is attached to you."

Her lashes flickered at his deliberate accusation. "That's to be expected. They all think I'm their long-lost cousin." She crossed her arms over her chest and lifted her chin. "Have you decided how you're going to break the news about me being an imposter?"

Paul forced air through his teeth in a soft hiss. "I'm not sure I can. The truth would crush Grady."

Her eyebrows went up in surprise. "What are you going to do then?"

"I don't know." He needed to discuss the situation with Ethan.

She narrowed her eyes in confusion. "So why did you want to talk to me?"

Why had he wanted to talk to her?

"I…"

What could he say? That she'd been on his mind the

entire time he was gone? That he found her fascinating despite his mistrust? He wanted to know everything about her. And not just because her mysterious background and limited digital footprint awakened his curiosity. Some of her behavior didn't fall into easily explainable patterns. For example, why did she dress up and visit children in the hospital? Something so altruistic was contrary to how an opportunist would behave. Unless she played on the sympathies of parents with sick children to some end. He'd never know unless he got to know her better.

And then there was the pesky physical attraction she inspired in him. Even now, as his thoughts took him down a somber path, he caught himself admiring her long lashes and wondering if her full lips could possibly be as soft as they looked. Her casual outfit showed off a toned body with soft curves. He imagined framing her slim hips with his hands and pulling her close. Dipping his head and running his lips down her neck to the place where it met her shoulder. Hearing her groan in pleasure as he lifted her against his growing erection and plunged his tongue into her mouth...

"Paul?" she said. "Are you okay?"

His name on her lips shocked him out of his lusty daydream. "No, I'm not okay. You and Ethan have put me in the untenable position of having to lie to Grady." A slight breeze flowed toward them from the garden, bringing the sweet scent of honeysuckle and cooling the heat beneath his skin.

"I know and I'm sorry." She put her hand on his arm and the contact seared him through two layers of fabric. "But you won't have to worry about that for too long. In a couple weeks, as soon as Grady is firmly on the road to a full recovery, we'll explain that the genetic testing place made a huge mistake and I'll be gone."

That she and his brother thought they could just snap their fingers and undo the whole situation showed just how impulsive they'd been.

"Why are you doing this?" he demanded, badly needing to understand. "What do you get out of it?"

Something flickered in her eyes briefly before she composed her features into an expression of benign innocence. "Nothing."

Nothing? Paul's muscles bunched as wariness returned. That didn't ring true. Because what he'd glimpsed in that microsecond was all the confirmation that he needed that Lia Marsh was up to no good.

Lia could tell Paul wasn't believing her claim and decided she'd better elaborate. "I really don't want anything from your grandfather or any of your family. I just want to help." She infused this last statement with all her passion, wondering if anything she said would quiet Paul's suspicions.

Earlier when she'd looked up and spied Paul standing in his grandfather's bedroom, her first reaction hadn't been panic, but vivid, undeniable lust. The guy was just so gorgeous. For someone who made his living thwarting cybercriminals he had an amazing physique. His broad shoulders and imposing height sent her heartbeat racing while his smoldering looks drove her desires into dangerous territory.

Now, as he frowned at her, Lia was struck again by

his sex appeal. Sunlight teased gold from his dark blond hair and highlighted his strong bone structure. In those all too brief moments when he wasn't scowling, his features were almost boyishly handsome, and Lia caught herself wishing he'd smile at her. A ridiculous wish considering that he'd made his opinion of her crystal clear.

Before Paul could respond, his phone rang. He glanced down at the screen and grimaced. "I have to take this."

The instant his attention shifted to the call, Lia retreated toward the house. She wanted to check in on Grady before heading back to her rental. Now that Paul had returned home, she decided the less time she spent around him the better for both of them.

As Lia neared the house, she spied Paul's mother descending the wrought iron staircase from the back terrace. Constance's welcoming smile gave Lia an unfamiliar sense of belonging that left her tongue-tied and riddled with guilt over her deception.

"There you are," Constance said. "Isn't Paul with you? Rosie said he'd been up to visit Grady."

"He had to take a call."

"It's probably his office. I swear that son of mine does nothing but work."

"Ethan said he's quite good at what he does."

"He's exceptionally good with computers and dedicated to running down criminals." For a moment Constance's clear blue eyes glowed with maternal fondness, then she sighed. "It caused quite a stir in our family when he opted to go work for the police department out of college rather than join Watts Shipping, but he needed to follow his heart."

"Catching crooks seems to be his passion."

"Yes, but it's grown into more of an obsession these last two years."

"How come?" Lia cursed her curiosity. She should be fighting her interest in the elder Watts brother not delving into his psyche.

"His friend's network services company was hacked and implanted with a bug that affected four million domains, causing them to leak sensitive customer data, including credit card details, for six months before it was discovered. The resulting bad press led to the company losing nearly all their major accounts and forced them out of business."

"Did Paul catch the hackers?"

"Eventually, but not soon enough to stop what happened to Ben."

Although she regretted that the topic had distressed Constance, Lia couldn't stop herself from wanting the whole story. "What happened to his friend?"

"After losing everything, he died in a terrible car accident." Constance's expression turned grim. "Paul thought the circumstances were suspicious because there were no other cars involved. Ben lost control, went off a bridge and drowned. Plus, there was a cryptic email Paul received shortly before the accident. Taken together, he thought perhaps Ben killed himself."

"That's awful."

Constance nodded. "Ben's death hit Paul really hard.

After that he became even more committed to shutting down hackers."

Sympathy for Paul momentarily pushed aside her wariness of him. At the same time she recognized this complex man had the power to turn her inside out.

"You know, I can't get over how much you look like your mother," Constance said, the abrupt shift of topic catching Lia off guard.

Lia knew her dark hair and hazel eyes set her apart from the blond and green-eyed Wattses, Ava included. She'd seen pictures of the woman. Yet on Ethan's word, the family had embraced her without question. At least most of them had.

"Tell me about her." Lia couldn't bring herself to say *my mother*.

"She was beautiful and talented." Constance's gaze turned inward. "She played tennis until she was fourteen at a level that she could've competed professionally."

"Why didn't she?"

"She had trouble staying focused on anything," Constance said. "By the time she hit her teenage years Ava was a handful. She grew up without a mother and Grady indulged her terribly. Everyone did because she could be charming when she set her mind to it."

"Ethan said after high school she headed to New York City to pursue modeling."

"She and Grady had a terrible row when he found out she didn't intend to go to college. He gave her a choice—get a degree or find a job. He had such high hopes for her future and wanted to motivate her." Constance sighed. "After years of no contact, Grady hired a private investigator to find her. That's when we learned she'd died. The police never contacted us because Ava did such a good job cutting her ties to Charleston. By the time we discovered Ava had given birth to you, you'd been adopted and the court records sealed."

"And my...father." The last word stuck in Lia's throat. Never mind her fake father—she knew nothing about her own father because her mother had refused to discuss him.

Constance blinked in surprise. "We don't know anything about him. Whatever your mother was up to in New York remains a complete mystery."

Both women lapsed into companionable silence, each occupied with her thoughts. Lia was wondering how to extricate herself without seeming rude when Paul's mother spoke again.

"It's so good to have you here," Constance declared with sudden vehemence. "I'm just sorry it took so long for us to find you."

"I had a good life." For some reason Lia felt compelled to defend her childhood. "A happy life."

"Of course you did," Constance said. "It's obvious that you're a loving, caring person. That sort of thing only happens if you've had the right upbringing. Your aunt Lenora and I were talking last night," Constance said, "and we think that you should move into your mother's old bedroom."

"Oh, well..." Overwhelmed by the thought of having to maintain her deception all the time, Lia scrambled for some polite way to refuse. "I couldn't impose."

"You're family. You wouldn't be imposing. And we

have purely selfish reasons to suggest it. We all feel that the more time you spend with Grady, the faster he'll improve."

"Yes, but…"

"He's been without you for too long. You two have a lot of catching up to do."

"Well, sure, but…"

"What are you two talking about?" Paul asked, coming up the gravel path behind them.

Lia turned to confront him, bracing herself for the heat of his displeasure when he found out what his mother had suggested.

"There you are," Constance said. "Rosie mentioned you'd arrived. Have you been up to see Grady? His progress is absolutely amazing."

"Quite amazing," Paul echoed, his distrustful green gaze flickering in Lia's direction.

"And we have Lia to thank."

"So I keep hearing," Paul muttered, his tone neutral.

Seeming unaware of the tension between her son and Lia, Constance continued, "I was just telling her that Lenora and I want her to move in."

"And I was just saying that I don't think that's a good idea," Lia inserted, hoping that he would give her credit for keeping his family at arm's length.

"There's no need to spend money on a rental when there's so much room here," Constance said.

"It's only for a couple weeks," Lia protested. "Then Misty and I will be on our way."

"Misty?" Paul asked.

"She's my camper trailer." She and Ethan had decided to stick close to her original story to avoid slipups.

"You named your camper Misty?" Paul interjected, his lips twisting sardonically.

Lia glared at him. He could insult her integrity all he wanted, but disparage her home and she'd come out swinging. "She's vintage."

Before Paul could reply, his mother jumped in. "Everyone is coming here to have dinner tonight. I hope you can make it."

"I came here straight from the airport," he said, "so I need to run home first."

"Take Lia. I'm sure she'd love to see your home. She's been cooped up with Grady for days. A little sea air would be good for her." Constance turned to Lia. "And on the way back you can pick up your things and get settled in."

"Really, I'm not sure…"

"It will be much better for Grady if you're close by."

Lia caved beneath Constance's firm determination. "Okay."

"Dinner is at seven," Paul's mother said.

"We'll be back in plenty of time." Paul hard gaze flicked to Lia as he bent to kiss his mother's cheek before striding off.

Lia hustled to catch up to him. As soon as they were out of earshot, she said, "I want you to know I didn't put her up to that."

"I know you didn't. Everyone believes what you've done for Grady is a miracle."

"I haven't done anything."

Paul surveyed her for several silent minutes before replying, "On the contrary. You've done plenty."

Despite his rampant disapproval, Paul demonstrated pristine Southern manners by opening the passenger door on his Range Rover and waiting while she climbed in before closing the door and circling to the driver's side.

"I know you aren't interested in spending any time with me so if you want to just drop me at my place—"

"On the contrary, I intend to spend our time away from the estate getting to know the real you."

It took Lia several panicky heartbeats to decide whether to be alarmed or thrilled. Obviously, he hadn't yet decided to go along with Ethan's wild scheme.

"Awesome." She managed the comeback without a trace of irony. "Does that go both ways?"

Paul stopped concentrating on the road and glanced her way. "What do you mean?"

"You want to know everything about me." Something reckless had taken ahold of her. "Are you going to let me get to know you, as well?"

"Why would you want to do that?" While Paul's tone remained neutral, a muscle bunched in his cheek.

"Because it's what normal people do. They exchange information and feel each other out."

Feel each other out? The phrase sounded flirtatious, and heaven knew she'd give anything if he'd just smile at her, but Paul didn't seem to hear it that way.

"Is that what you did with Ethan?" The tightness in his voice took her aback.

"Why would you ask about him?"

"I still can't figure out your relationship with my brother. How much is he paying you for this little charade?"

Now she understood where Paul was going with his questions. "He agreed to cover what I'm losing in income for a couple weeks."

"How much?" Paul asked.

"I don't know." Lia scrunched up her face as she calculated. "No week is the same. I get paid by the client and that varies."

"Ballpark it for me."

"Including tips, it averages to about eight hundred dollars a week."

For the first time Paul looked taken aback. "That's it?"

Spoken like a man who drove a luxury SUV and lived at the beach. No doubt he couldn't fathom Lia's frugal ways any more than she understood paying more for a single pair of shoes than it cost her to eat for an entire month.

"That's it." Lia believed in the equitable exchange of money for goods or services. "All I want is what's fair."

Paul gave her a skeptical look. "What if I paid you fifty thousand dollars to go away and never come back?"

For several seconds Lia pondered the fancy truck she could buy with such an enormous sum. For six months she'd been stuck in Charleston while she saved enough to replace her wrecked vehicle. Accepting Paul's outrageous offer would enable her to return to her nomadic lifestyle in a few days.

"You said you wanted to get to know me better," she said. "Well, the first thing you should know is that I'm not motivated by money."

"Which is exactly what you'd say," Paul countered, "if your endgame would guarantee you a greater pay-out."

"Are you suspicious of me in particular or people in general?"

"You have to see that I have good reason to doubt you," he said.

"I really don't see it at all," she shot back, wishing that he'd stop toying with her.

Did he know about her past? Bile rose in her throat as she imagined his disgust. But if he'd dug up her secrets, he'd confront her directly. She studied his profile while her heart thundered in her ears and realized that fearing that he knew all about her background was making her come across as guilty. Lia breathed in for a count of four and released the air just as slowly. What did it matter if Paul knew her story? His good opinion shouldn't matter to her.

Paul studied her the whole time she was striving for calm. "You didn't answer me about taking fifty thousand to disappear."

Lia considered what her mother's reaction would have been to Paul's offer. Jen Marsh had a complicated relationship with money and many of her attitudes had rubbed off on her daughter. Lia lived frugally, avoiding debt, buying only what she needed, living with less stuff. But Jen Marsh took her disdain for spending one step beyond obsessive after what she'd experienced growing up.

"You don't have to pay me anything to drop this whole charade and vanish from your lives," Lia said, noticing a subtle easing in the tension around Paul's mouth. The desire to gain his trust prompted her to add, "Whatever you and Ethan decide is fine with me."

Four

"So you'd really go?" Even as he asked the question, Paul recognized exposing her would throw his whole family into chaos. "If I convinced Ethan that you should?"

"Yes." She cocked her head and studied him. "Frankly I'm surprised you haven't done so already."

"He's not taking my calls."

Paul gripped the steering wheel and contemplated Lia's declaration. Would she really leave the decision up to him and Ethan or would she act behind the scenes to win Ethan to her side?

"So you don't know."

"Don't know what?" Paul asked, wondering what else had gone wrong in his absence.

"How this whole situation came about."

Paul glanced her way. "And how's that?"

"Ethan put me in a position where the only choices I had were to go along and pretend to be Grady's granddaughter or tell the truth and risk that he might not recover from the blow."

Although he wasn't surprised that she'd blame the whole situation on Ethan, Paul asked, "Why don't you tell me what happened."

"Ethan set me up. I thought I was visiting Grady as myself. Instead as I stood beside his bed and held his hand, both he and Ethan ambushed me with this whole thing about being Ava's daughter."

"So you're blaming my grandfather for this situation, as well?"

"No. Yes. Sort of. Ethan told me Grady came up with the idea on his own."

"You didn't mention that Grady might be inspired to improve if his granddaughter miraculously appeared?"

Lia's mouth dropped open. "To what end?"

"The Wattses are a wealthy, old Charleston family. We wield both power and influence in this town. You might've liked the idea of being a part of that."

"Hardly," she sniffed. "In fact, it sounds stressful and intimidating. Not to mention having the threat of a simple DNA test hanging over my head all the time."

"Yet here you are." Distracted by their conversation, Paul almost missed the turnoff to Sullivan's Island. "And here I am. Damn it. I hate having to lie to everyone in my family, but most of all to Grady."

"I feel the same way. Your mom and aunt have been welcoming. And your cousins are really nice. It's horrible that I can't be truthful, but then I see how happy

Grady is and watch him get a little better every day, and I think the whole messed-up situation might work out okay."

Paul refused to be persuaded by her feel-good justification. "I'm sure this is the logic you and Ethan have used to justify what you've done, but lying is wrong."

"A lot of the time it is, but not always. What about lying to protect someone's feelings? As long as the lie isn't malicious it doesn't do any harm."

It all sounded like a bunch of excuses to Paul, but he'd invited her on this trip to his house to gain insight into her and this conversation was teaching him a lot. "So you don't believe the truth can set you free?"

"Not always. Sometimes it can be painful."

"That doesn't justify lying."

Lia shrugged. "We will just have to agree to disagree."

Paul glanced her way and saw that she was staring out the passenger window at the passing landscape. Despite their opposing opinions, he couldn't shake his fascination with her.

"I guess we will."

An unrelenting silence fell between them that didn't break even as Paul turned the SUV into his driveway and stopped before his house. Switching off the engine, he glanced her way. Lia radiated disappointment and hurt, but Paul refused to be drawn in. Despite her positive effect on Grady, Paul couldn't shake the notion that Lia Marsh was going to cause trouble for his family.

She was working an angle. He just needed to figure out what it was. Which was why he'd decided to move into the carriage house, located near the back of the estate, for the next two weeks so he could keep an eye on her. He intended for Lia to understand that he wasn't taken in by her do-gooder act.

"I'll just be a few minutes," he said. "Do you want to wait here or come in?"

"I'm sure you'd prefer I stay here."

He dismissed her sarcasm with a shrug. "Suit yourself."

But as he headed up the stairs to his front door, he heard her footsteps on the wood boards behind him. The electronic lock on the entrance disengaged as he neared. He opened the door and gestured Lia inside. After suggesting she check out the view, Paul left Lia gawking at the beach beyond the towering floor-to-ceiling windows that made up one wall of his spacious great room. In his bedroom, he unpacked his luggage, swapping the tailored suits he'd worn to the conference for the slacks and button-down shirts he favored for the office.

Before he'd done more than replace his suits in the closet and dump his dirty clothes into the hamper, Paul's phone began to ring. He glanced at the screen, saw Ethan's name and the disquiet he'd been feeling at his brother's snub eased slightly.

Despite their family's expectations, it was Ethan and not Paul who was following in Grady's footsteps as family mediator and key decision maker. Ethan had always been the empathetic brother. Outgoing and social, he tended to be more in touch with the emotions. And despite being the younger brother, everyone turned to Ethan for advice and support.

In contrast, Paul was more comfortable as a lone wolf. He liked technology because of its logic and predictability and had chosen to become a cop because he thrived on the challenge of catching criminals. That doing so also helped people was a bonus, but it didn't drive him. No doubt Ethan would say this attitude made him a jerk.

Would Lia agree?

Paul couldn't imagine what made the question pop into his mind. Nor did he care about some interloper's opinion about him.

"It's about time you called me back," Paul said irritably into the phone, closing the master bedroom door in case Lia decided to eavesdrop.

"Before you go all big brother and start lecturing me about how much I messed up, tell me you don't see a huge change in Grady."

"Fine. I'll admit that Grady's better and that believing Lia is Ava's daughter is the reason, but why the hell did you drag me into it by saying I'm the one who found her?"

"I thought if you got the credit for doing something that would make Grady incredibly happy that it would repair your relationship."

"You're wrong to hope that will make me less furious with you for dragging me into your scheme." Yet even as he spoke, Paul's heart clenched. Despite the tension that had grown between the brothers, Paul appreciated that Ethan had his back. "Have you thought this whole thing through? He's going to be devastated when the truth comes out. And it will because there's no way I'm letting this go on."

"I didn't figure you would, but he'll be stronger in a few weeks." Ethan paused for a heartbeat. "Or she doesn't have to go anywhere." When Paul sucked in a breath to protest, Ethan jumped in. "Hear me out. She spends all her time driving around the country in a vintage camper picking up odd jobs wherever she goes. That's no life. Instead she could stay with us and be our cousin."

"Have you lost your mind?" Paul demanded, wondering what sort of madness had overcome his brother. "We don't know anything about this person."

"I do. She's genuine and kind. Everyone loves her."

"Even you?"

"What?" Ethan exclaimed, following it up with a rough laugh. "Hardly."

Unsatisfied by his brother's answer, Paul asked another. "Is she in love with you?"

"No."

Paul hadn't been entirely satisfied by Lia's denials and he sensed Ethan was holding something back. While it wasn't unusual for Ethan to champion something or someone he believed in, the level of trust he'd afforded Lia compelled Paul to take nothing for granted.

"Are you sure?" Paul pondered the amount of time Lia had undoubtedly spent with her hands roaming over Ethan's naked body. While she'd claimed to be a professional massage therapist, there was something overtly intimate about the experience. "Women tend to fall for you rather quickly."

"That's because I'm nice to them." Ethan's tone was dry as he finished, "You should try it sometime."

For a second Paul didn't know how to respond to his brother's dig. In truth, he had neither time nor interest in a personal life these days. His consulting company grew busier each year as criminals became increasingly bolder and more clever. Technology changed faster than most people could keep up and new threats emerged daily.

On the other hand, Ethan had taken on more responsibility since their grandfather's stroke compelled their father to pick up Grady's chairmanship duties. Although Ethan had been groomed for years to take over one day, having the responsibility thrust on him without any transition period had increased the amount of hours Ethan spent at the office by 50 percent. Yet he still carved out time for family and friends, dating and even attending their mother's endless charity events.

Paul just didn't want to put in the effort. He'd always been solitary, preferring intimate gatherings with his small circle of friends versus the active bar scene or loud parties. Her solitary lifestyle was probably the one thing Paul actually understood about Lia Marsh.

"Are you sure Lia didn't put the idea in your head that she should play the part of Ava's daughter?"

"Trust me—I came up with the plan all on my own."

Paul gave a noncommittal grunt. "She claims she's only planning on sticking around for two weeks." He paused, assessing how much damage would be done during that span.

"That's what we agreed to. I tried to convince her to

stay for a month, but she's determined to go. She doesn't like staying anywhere for more than a few months."

"What's up with that?"

"I don't know. She doesn't talk much about herself."

Paul considered his earlier conversation with Lia. "You don't think that indicates she has something to hide?" While he waited for Ethan to respond, Paul relived his joy in Grady's affectionate greeting. The thought of losing his grandfather's love and approval all over again filled Paul with dread. "Okay, I really hate the situation, but I agree that she's had a positive impact on Grady. As long as it's only two weeks, I'm okay if she stays around and pretends to be Ava's daughter."

"Thanks." Ethan released the word on a long exhale as if he'd been holding his breath. "And don't worry, we've figured out an exit strategy. It's all going to work out. You'll see."

"Both of you keep saying the same thing. I hope like hell that you're right."

"We are." Ethan's smile came through loud and clear. "And be nice to Lia. She's doing us a huge favor."

After he'd hung up with Ethan, Paul chewed over his brother's final statement as he tossed what clothes he'd need for the next two weeks into a duffel. No one would question his decision to stay at the estate. His office was a few blocks away. He'd slept in the carriage house often since Grady's stroke and even before that had utilized the cozy apartment to break for a nap during an intense case when an hour-long round-trip drive to his beach house was time he couldn't afford.

Paul dropped his overnight bag in the foyer and returned to the great room in search of Lia. He looked out the window and saw her standing beside the pool, her arms crossed over her chest, her attention fixed on the Atlantic Ocean. She'd freed her hair and the brisk wind off the water turned the dark strands into a fluttering pennant. He went out to join her.

"I've never been able to decide if I prefer the mountains or the beach," she said, her lips curving into a smile. "I guess that's why I travel so much. There are always new places to discover."

Her tranquil expression transfixed him. He surveyed the freckles dusting her nose and upper cheeks and wondered what about her captivated him. Was it the thrill of the hunt? He'd parlayed his passion for tracking down cybercriminals into a multimillion-dollar company. Lia presented the exact sort of mystery that drove him to work seventy- and eighty-hour weeks to keep his clients' data safe.

And yet here he was, compelled to accept a suspicious stranger as his cousin in order to save his grandfather. Despite Ethan's assurances, Paul knew Lia represented a danger to his family.

So with that foremost in his mind, why did he constantly find himself fighting the urge to touch her? To sample the warmth of her skin. To pull her tight against him and capture her rosy lips in a heated kiss. This unrelenting war between his body and mind was as exhausting as it was troubling.

Had she influenced Ethan the same way? From their earlier conversation Ethan made it clear he trusted Lia. Before she came along, Paul never questioned his brother's judgment. What was it about Lia that roused Paul's suspicions?

"I think my brother might be in love with you."

"What?" She tore her attention from the view and huffed out a laugh. "That's ridiculous."

"Is it?" Paul countered. "He's very protective of you."

"That's because he likes me." Lia turned and studied his expression for several seconds before adding, "I'm a nice person."

Paul's nostrils flared. "Are you sleeping with him?"

"He's my client," she shot back. "I don't sleep with clients."

"But you're attracted to him?"

"He has an incredible body," she mused, with reckless disregard for his escalating annoyance. "Great muscles. Shoulders to die for. Strong thighs." She paused as if taking stock of the impact her words were having. "And as a massage therapist I have to say it's nice when a man takes such good care of his skin."

"So you are attracted to him?"

Lia gave an impatient snort. "Ethan has impeccable manners, a deep, sexy drawl and an overabundance of charm. That I'm not the least bit attracted to him made my coworkers—of both sexes—question my sexual orientation. I'm a professional. I never would've kept Ethan as a client if he'd inspired even a trace of lust. That sort of thing crosses a line for me."

"You forget I've seen you two together. There's something between you."

"He's felt comfortable enough with me to share stuff," she murmured.

"There's more to it than that."

"No, there isn't," Lia declared impatiently before sucking in a deep, calming breath. "Look," she said, giving her shoulders a little shake to relax them. "I feel as if we're dancing around something."

"I don't dance."

"No," Lia muttered wryly. "I expect you don't. Look, for this to work, we really need to find a way to get along." She paused, giving him the opportunity to agree. When he remained silent, Lia chose not to wait him out. "How about if I confess something that's hard for me to admit?" She cleared her throat and gave a nervous half smile. "I find you attractive."

He should've regarded the admission as a clever manipulation and met it with skepticism. Instead, her confession lit up his body like a fireworks finale.

"Why would you tell me something like that?"

"It gives you a little power over me," she said with a sexy, sweet smile that sent an electric pulse zipping along his nerve endings.

"And you think I need that," he countered, bothered that she had him all figured out. Well, maybe not all figured out. But she had a pretty good idea of what made him tick. It served as a reminder that he needed to stay on his guard around her.

"Don't you?" Her presumptive manner bordered on overconfidence. "I think you crave being in control at all times and I'll bet it drives you crazy when things don't go according to plan."

"I don't go crazy," he said, stepping into her space,

unwilling to consider his real motivation for what he was about to do. "I adapt."

Lia misjudged the reason Paul closed the gap between them and never saw the kiss coming. Being caught completely by surprise heightened the emotional impact of his soft breath feathering across her skin. An instant later, his lips touched hers and a million stars exploded behind her eyelids. He cradled her head with strong fingers, grounding her while the firm, masterful pressure of his mouth stole her breath and her equilibrium.

Paul's kisses were in a class all by themselves. Never before had she been so swept up in the magic of the moment. The perfection of his lips gliding over hers. The hitch in his breath as she shifted her weight onto her toes and leaned in to him. Lia never wanted the kiss to end, but couldn't explain why. What was it about Paul that called to her? He'd offered her nothing but skepticism and scowls. Yet the clean, masculine scent of him, the gentle sweep of his fingertips against her skin unleashed both joy and hunger.

When he sucked on her bottom lip, she groaned and gave him full access to her mouth. His tongue swept against hers and the taste of him only increased her appetite for more. Lia tunneled her fingers into his hair to keep their mouths fused as he fed on her lips and she devoured him in turn.

His arm banded around her waist, drawing her snugly against his hard torso. While she'd appreciated Paul's powerful body from a safe distance, pressed like this against the unyielding solidity of his strong abs sharpened the longing to feel his weight settle over her.

She'd been kissed enough to recognize she'd never experienced anything like this before. Where moments ago she'd been shivering in the cool breeze coming off the ocean, now her skin burned as fire raced through her veins and sent heat deep into her loins. Paul must've recognized the upward tick in her passion because his hand curved over her butt and squeezed just hard enough to send a jolt of pleasure lancing between her thighs. She gasped and arched her back, driving her breasts against him to satisfy their craving for contact.

His fingers tightened on her, the grip almost bruising, and then he was breaking off the kiss and relaxing his hold. Lia might've cried out in protest, but an icy lash of sea wind struck her overheated flesh, wrenching her back to reality. She shifted a half step back, surprised at the unsteadiness of her knees. Setting her hand on Paul's chest for balance, she noted his rough exhalation. Her own heart was pumping hard in the aftermath of the kiss.

She looked up and caught a glimpse of the twin green flames flickering in his eyes. A moment later all trace of heat vanished from his gaze. Had she imagined it? As much as it pained her to leave the warmth and comfort of his embrace, Lia needed distance to gather her thoughts and make sense of what had just happened. Paul had made it crystal clear that he didn't like her. So, what was he doing?

"Was that meant to determine whether I was telling the truth about being attracted to you?" Lia panted, scanning Paul's expression and hoping that wasn't what the kiss had been about.

"Why would you think I'd do that?" he countered, dragging his thumb over his lower lip.

Mesmerized by the action, Lia shivered as pleasurable aftershocks continued to rock her body. "Because you don't believe anything I say." The bitterness in her tone caught her by surprise. She wished Paul's good opinion wasn't so important to her. "So what's the verdict? Do you think I'm attracted to you?"

"Yes." He waited a beat for her retort. When none came, he raised his eyebrows. "Aren't you going to ask me if the feeling's mutual?"

Lia shook her head and forced her muscles to relax. "I don't want to play those sorts of games with you."

Paul's features looked carved in granite as he regarded her. "I told Ethan I will go along with your subterfuge for now."

"Great." Lia slumped in defeat, unsure why this news bothered her so much. Had she really hoped he'd call her out in front of his family and drive her away? Given who he was, what he believed in, he should. "I'm sure that made Ethan very happy," she murmured.

Paul scrutinized her for several seconds before nodding. "We should be getting back."

The ride to Charleston passed with little conversation between them. Lia needed to sort out her feelings about the kiss, Paul's abrupt acceptance of her temporarily posing as his long-lost cousin and what would happen if her reasons for playing the part ever came to light.

Already Lia suspected her strong attraction to Paul

could develop into an emotional attachment unlike anything she'd known before. She'd never experienced such an unshakable craving to be with anyone. The need scared her a little, but the compelling nature of her desire was impossible to ignore. She couldn't pretend that surrendering to temptation wouldn't have repercussions. Lia couldn't imagine this longing for him would just vanish one day. Even if Paul never found out where she came from and rejected her, she planned to get back on the road in a matter of weeks. For her future peace of mind, she needed to bottle up her feelings here and now.

Yet what was going on between her and Paul wasn't the only emotional time bomb ticking away. The way Paul's mother and aunt had welcomed her into the family had touched Lia in a way she hadn't expected. Despite her guilt at the fraud she was perpetrating on them, the love they'd shown for their missing niece left Lia pondering what her own homecoming might be if she ever reached out to the family her mother left behind in Seattle.

Jen Marsh had struck out on her own shortly after high school and never looked back. Reluctance to linger in any place for long meant she rarely formed any lasting attachments. And neither had Lia.

But even though she lacked experience with lasting familial support, sometimes Lia pined for a family to belong to. Not that she imagined fitting into a large, tight-knit group like the Wattses. The reality was slowly sinking in that she would soon be living amongst them and that they would expect her to share their limelight. Jen Marsh had gone to great lengths to escape her past and create an anonymous life for both her and Lia.

If Paul kept digging into her background, could he jeopardize that? Would a story about the granddaughter of a swindler interest anyone three decades after he went to jail? Doubtful. But to be sure, she'd better avoid any public attention for the next two weeks.

After a brief stop at her rental to pack up her limited wardrobe, Paul drove straight back to the estate. Constance must've been on the lookout for them because she was on hand in the first-floor hallway to lead the way upstairs to the bedrooms, narrating as she went.

"The Birch-Watts House has six bedrooms and seven bathrooms," Constance said. "It was built in 1804 by Jacob Birch and his descendants lived here until 1898 when Theodore Watts bought it. The home's been in the Watts family ever since."

"Wow, that's a long time." Lia had been present when they'd brought Grady home from the hospital and had been too focused on getting him settled to take in much more than a cursory impression of the grand mansion. "And only Ethan's grandfather lives here?"

It seemed like a lot of empty space for just one person to rattle around in. A house with nearly ten thousand square feet and so many bedrooms should be full of people. And in its heyday, it probably was. But families were smaller now and not so likely to have several generations living under one roof.

"Grady's been alone since he lost Grandma back in the late 1960s," Paul added, "but the Shaw twins live in the caretaker's house on the back corner of the estate. And I spend the night in the carriage house here and there. More often since his stroke."

"He must like having you all close by," Lia murmured, realizing she might be inundated with family members over the next week.

"Both girls are so busy with their careers and social lives." Constance sighed. "Which is why it's wonderful that you've come to spend time with Grady. Did you bring a swimsuit? The pool was recently refurbished and switched to salt water."

"No, I didn't think it was going to be that sort of a visit." Seeing Paul's lips tighten, Lia suppressed a twinge of regret. No matter what he thought, she had no intention of treating her time with his family like a vacation. She intended to do her best to get Grady as healthy as possible in the next two weeks.

"This was your mother's room." Constance led the way into the room on the opposite side of the hall from Grady's master suite. "It's the best guest room in the house."

"Wow!"

The enormous, bright bedroom overlooked the gardens and side lawn with floral curtains framing the four tall windows set into the muted green walls. Lia's gaze darted from the view to the big bed with its matching comforter and the yellow fainting couch at its foot. A giant mirrored armoire dominated one wall and Lia knew without even opening the doors that even with the two bulky costumes she'd brought along, her clothes wouldn't take up half the space.

"You sound like you approve," Constance declared with a delighted smile.

"I've never stayed anywhere so nice. Or so big," Lia said. "It's more space than I'm used to."

Lia was a minimalist by necessity as well as desire. The friends she'd made during her travels marveled at how little she needed, but Lia had never known any other way to be. Traveling around the country in a nineteen-foot camper meant owning a bare minimum of essentials. The only deviation from that rule was her ever expanding collection of princess costumes.

Yet the moment she'd entered the bedroom, Lia had been blown away by the beautiful antiques, the intricate plasterwork around the ceiling and fireplace, the ridiculously comfortable-looking bed and the bathroom that was bigger than her entire camper. For several long seconds she imagined herself spending long hours soaking in the tub. Then reality intruded. She wasn't on vacation. A couple weeks from now she and Misty would be back on the road.

"Get used to it," Constance advised. "You're going to be with us for a long time."

"Um…"

Turbulent emotions rose up in Lia, tightening her throat and making it impossible to speak. Being thrust into the tight-knit Watts family highlighted the isolation in her lifestyle and brought her into direct conflict with her mother's attitude that just because someone was family didn't mean they gave a damn about you.

"Paul, can you go let Cory know he needs to bring up the rest of Lia's things?"

"This is all there is," Paul answered, setting the boxes containing her costumes on the bed.

"What do you mean?" Constance looked from the

boxes to the small duffel that held most of Lia's wardrobe. "How is that possible?"

"Not everyone requires an entire room to hold every outfit they own," Paul remarked dryly.

His mother looked mystified. "But…"

"I don't have much room in my camper," Lia explained. "And I don't really need much."

"That was your life before. You are a Watts now and should dress the part." Constance cast a dubious eye over Lia's yoga pants and T-shirt. "We need to get you some new clothes. The twins can show you all their favorite boutiques."

"There's no need," Lia said, shooting a wary glance in Paul's direction. He would hate that his mother wanted to spend money on her. But his impassive expression tossed her no lifeline. "I'm sure Poppy and Dallas are too busy to take me shopping. Besides, I'm only going to be here a couple weeks."

"Nonsense. You simply have to stay longer than that. Because of you, Grady is getting better every day. No need for you to stay cooped up in the house all the time. The twins and Ethan can take you out so you can meet their friends. I have several events in the next two weeks that all of us will be attending. When word gets around all of Charleston will be dying to meet you."

As Constance spoke, Lia's anxiety ratcheted upward. Chest tightening, on the verge of a mild panic attack, she made another silent appeal to Paul. Why hadn't he spoken up? Surely he'd rather she stay out of sight between now and the time they broke the news that she wasn't a Watts after all. Once again, he remained utterly silent and aloof. Her eyebrows dipped as she realized his refusal to step in was deliberate. He was withholding aid in order to demonstrate the folly of Ethan's plan. As if she needed that pointed out to her.

"I'm feeling really overwhelmed at the moment," Lia protested. "I'm not used to so much attention. If you don't mind, I'd like to focus on helping Grady get better."

"Oh, well, of course." Constance looked surprised and then a bit abashed. "I guess I went a little overboard. We're just so overjoyed to have you home."

At long last Paul took pity on Lia. "Mother, why don't we leave Lia to unpack."

The grateful look she shot him prompted a frown. Honestly, there seemed to be no way to get on the man's good side.

"Of course," Constance said, her gracious smile returning. "Join us downstairs when you're ready." She'd taken several steps toward the door when she suddenly stopped and turned. "I almost forgot. There's a little welcome-home present for you on the nightstand."

Lia's first reaction after glancing at Paul's set expression was to protest that she didn't need any gifts. Then she realized that she could leave behind whatever they gave her. "That's lovely. Thank you."

Left alone, she started to fill the dresser drawers with her meager belongings, but then succumbed to curiosity about the gift. A small, flat box sat beside an elegant sheet of linen notepaper.

This belonged to your grandmother. We thought you should have it.—Constance.

Lia slipped the ribbon off the box and opened it. Nestled on a bed of black velvet was an antique locket. Her heart contracted as she opened the locket and saw that it contained a picture of Ava as a teenager. She sank onto the bed and stared at the photo, pondering all the events that had led her to this moment, wishing she'd done a dozen things differently.

"Hey."

Lia lifted her gaze and spied Ethan standing in the doorway. He looked authoritative in an elegant navy suit and lavender tie.

"Hi."

"Are you okay about staying at the estate for the next two weeks?" Ethan asked as he entered. "Both my mom and Aunt Lenora can be very determined and I don't want you to feel pressured."

Lia blew out her breath. "I plan to spend most of my time with your grandfather so I should be able to handle it for a couple weeks."

Ethan came over and took her hand in his. "I know this isn't what we originally planned on. I owe you a huge debt for helping out like this."

"You really don't," Lia said, some of her angst melting away. "I just want to bring your family some peace."

"You'll definitely be doing that."

"Can you please talk your mom out of introducing me all over Charleston as Ava's daughter, though? That's just going to end up complicating everything and I don't think you want your family to be the subject of gossip."

"Sure, that makes sense." Ethan tugged at the knot on his tie, loosening it. "I'll deal with it."

"Thank you because your brother was no help. I thought for sure he'd want to keep me out of sight."

"I know it's hard to believe, but I think that Paul will come around once he gets to know you."

"I hope so." The memory of their kiss sent heat rushing into her cheeks. Longing spiraled through her. "Because it's daunting how much he dislikes me."

Five

With the successful completion of a year-long investigation into a data breach of one of his company's clients, Paul knocked off early and headed to the estate to see how Grady was doing. Before Lia Marsh had entered their lives, Paul rarely worked a standard eight-hour day. He loved what he did and despite the number of bad actors he and his staff tracked down, there was always another puzzle to unravel, another hacker who'd stolen information. But these days he couldn't concentrate on his day-to-day activities.

When he wasn't following the trail she'd left all over the country, he caught himself ruminating over that stolen moment at his beach house when he'd surrendered to his desire to kiss her. At various times over the last several days, he'd have given anything to escape the distracting memory of how she'd felt in his arms. To forget the softness of her lips as they'd yielded beneath his. To stop imagining his hands gliding over her silky, fragrant skin.

He'd intended for the impulsive act to rattle her, but the aftermath hadn't offered him any insight into her nefarious plans. Nor in the last week had she made any misstep to confirm she wasn't as genuine as she appeared. The dry facts that summarized her life gave him no sense of her character or her motivation for interrupting her life to act as Grady's granddaughter. He hadn't yet ruled out money, but nothing about the way she dressed or the things she talked about gave her away.

It also occurred to Paul that maybe he was concerning himself with the wrong thing. With only a week left to go in their arrangement, Grady continued to improve. But once they told everyone their story that a mistake had been made at the genetic testing service and Lia wasn't his granddaughter, would Grady's health fade once more?

There was no doubt that her presence had galvanized his recovery, but neither Paul nor Ethan could predict whether Grady's progress would slow or stop when she left the following week. Lia persisted in her belief that once she'd gotten the ball rolling, Grady would continue to improve on his own, but what if she was the oxygen that kept the flame burning on Grady's will to return to full health?

Paul stepped out of his SUV, intending to head straight to the carriage house for a cold beer and more brooding about Lia, when he spotted a flash of yellow coming toward him along the garden path. If he retreated without saying hello to whoever was coming, he'd never hear the end of it. Even as that zipped through his mind, he registered the sound of humming above the crunch of gravel and recognized the source.

Lia.

After that stirring kiss at his house, he'd avoided being alone with her, and he cursed at this untimely meeting. But the woman who emerged from the foliage had a completely different impact on him than what he was used to.

What the hell?

Before he could wrap his mind around her appearance, Lia spotted him and waved. Her infectious smile bloomed as she headed in his direction. His head spun as he took her in. She'd transformed herself into yet another one of her princess characters. Even her movement was different.

"What are you wearing?" he asked, regaining his voice.

"It's a ball gown," she responded as if it was the most ordinary thing in the world to be wearing a floor-length satin and tulle dress in bright yellow with three voluminous tiers, a red wig styled in a fancy updo with ringlets spilling over her bare shoulders and long yellow gloves. "I'm on my way to the hospital to visit the children's ward. I've been so busy with Grady that I missed last week and I can't disappoint them again."

Paul groaned inwardly. It was hard to maintain his skepticism about her when this woman kept proving him wrong. First, she'd brought his grandfather back from the brink of death. Now here was another reminder that she gave of her time to bring joy to sick kids. How was he supposed to resist her?

"Which princess are you today?"

"I'm dressed as Belle. From *Beauty and the Beast*," she explained with exaggerated patience. "The Disney movie about the prince who was turned into a beast and could only be saved by someone who loved him as himself." When Paul continued blankly regarding her, she rolled her eyes in exasperation. "I can tell you don't have children."

"Why do you dress like a Disney character?"

"Because the kids love it. Sure, they appreciate when I just show up to spend time with them, but when I visit dressed as Belle or Elsa or Cinderella…they are so thrilled." She grinned. "For a while they can forget how sick they are."

"How did you get started doing this?"

"I guess you could say growing up I wanted to be a princess. I imagined that I was like Rapunzel or Sleeping Beauty, locked in a tower taken away from my parents. Hidden away. When I got older, I grew obsessed with getting a job at Disney as one of the princesses."

"So what happened?"

"I became a Disney character." She made a face that told him it had not gone well. "Only I didn't get to be a princess."

"A villain?" he asked, thinking that would be more fun.

"No," she said. "I was Dale." She waited a beat and when he didn't say anything, elaborated, "Of Chip 'n' Dale. They were chipmunks. I wore a big chipmunk head." She used her hands to indicate the costume's size. "It was hot and uncomfortable, but mostly worth it because the kids loved it."

"How did you make the transition from Disney character to massage therapist?" he asked, the thought of her massaging his brother once again flashing unpleasantly through his mind. He recognized that she'd been baiting him when they discussed it, but still he envied his brother.

"I think I mentioned it was hot and stuffy in that costume. Being a character wasn't as glamorous as I'd hoped it would be. One of my coworkers was taking classes in massage therapy and it sounded like a good idea. It was a way for me to help people and that's what I like to do."

"Well, you've certainly had a huge impact on Grady, so I guess you have a knack for making people better."

"Thank you for saying that," she said, showing her appreciation with a bright smile that kicked him hard in the gut.

"How are you getting there?"

"I'm going to walk." She shifted sideways as if to go around him. "It's only fifteen minutes away."

Paul stepped to block her path. "Why don't I drive you instead?"

"Really," she demurred. "It's no problem."

"I insist," he argued, faltering in his week-long battle to avoid being alone with her.

"I like walking."

"So do I. I could walk you there."

She set her hands on her hips and arched one eyebrow. "Don't you have evildoers to chase?"

"Nope. We just wrapped up a huge investigation so I took the afternoon off." Paul held out his arm to her in a gallant gesture that caught her by surprise. "I can't think of anything I'd enjoy more than to watch your performance as Belle."

"But I'm usually there for a couple hours. I'm sure you have better things to do."

"Stop trying to get rid of me," he growled. "There's nothing else I'd rather be doing." And much to his dismay, that was true.

Although she looked like she wanted to voice further protests, Lia gave a little shrug and took his arm. Her delicate grip made such a huge impression that Paul had a hard time concentrating as she told him the story of how Belle and the Beast fell in love.

Fifteen minutes had never gone by so quickly, and all too soon Paul was guiding Lia through the hospital's entrance. Gliding along the corridors, she paid little attention to the stir she caused. The staff greeted her warmly, but Paul couldn't help but notice the way many visitors goggled at her appearance or even laughed at her elaborate costume. He caught himself scowling at a number of them even as he recalled his own initial reaction when he first saw her.

"What?" he demanded, noticing her amused expression as they stood waiting for the elevator to arrive.

"I was just thinking that the way you're glaring makes me think you'd make an excellent Beast."

He forced his facial muscles to relax. "I don't suppose I'm Prince Charming material."

"You could be," she murmured, stepping into the elevator car.

"No," he corrected. "Ethan is Prince Charming." A now-familiar pulse of irritation raised his blood pressure.

"Ethan?" Her snort was an indelicate sound at odds with her royal appearance. "Do you really see him dressing up in britches and a frock coat?"

Not in his wildest imaginings. Paul's lips twitched, but he kept his tone serious. "Maybe for the right woman."

She gave another very unprincesslike snort. "I don't think he'd enjoy playacting."

"I wouldn't, either."

She narrowed her glowing hazel eyes and shot him a piercing glance. "You might be surprised."

Her knowing smile sent a wave of heat through him. Before he could summon a retort, the doors opened and Lia stepped into the corridor of what was obviously the children's floor. She paused for a second, drew in a deep breath, closed her eyes. A moment later, she exhaled and a beatific smile curved her lips. Just like that she'd become someone completely different.

The transformation robbed Paul of words. He trailed after her as she approached the nurses' station and after greeting everyone, introduced Paul. Several nurses accompanied them on the way to the lounge where some of the children had gathered to play. The appearance of a beloved princess in their midst electrified the children.

Mesmerized by the spectacle, Paul stood at the back of the room with a cluster of parents and watched Lia work her way around the space, going from child to child, spreading joy as she went. Some of the kids she called by name, proving that she was indeed a frequent visitor. In every case she lingered, answering questions, asking some of her own.

Nor was Lia's effect limited to the kids. Around Paul several stressed-out mothers teared up at their children's delight and tense fathers relaxed enough to smile. Once again, Lia was demonstrating the incredible magic she'd used to wrest Grady away from the brink of death.

Paul noticed a tightness in his chest and rubbed to ease it. This woman was too much. He recalled Ethan declaring that first day that Lia came off as completely genuine. Confident his brother had been hoodwinked, Paul had done whatever he could to unmask her. Now he was leaning toward her giving her the benefit of the doubt. This hospital visit was the whip cream, sprinkles and cherry on top of the ice cream sundae that was Lia Marsh.

Which made everything so much worse.

Keeping his attraction to her buttoned down had been way easier when he had reason to suspect her character and motives. Now, as she began to sing, Paul's spirits sank. Her clear, sweet voice captivated the children. Their parents looked beyond grateful to see their sons and daughters so happy. And some of the nursing staff were singing along.

Before her topsy-turvy world had intersected with his, Paul never would've imagined himself attracted to a free spirit like Lia. Her ideas about the rejuvenating effects of music and aromatherapies seemed more like wishful thinking than practical fact. Yet he couldn't deny Grady's marked improvement.

Or his own shifting opinion.

Over the next hour Lia demonstrated an extensive repertoire of familiar children's songs. When at long last she signaled the end of the performance with a princess-worthy curtsy and waved goodbye, Paul wasn't surprised at the sharp tug his heart gave when she shifted her full attention to him.

"Sorry that took so long," she said as they headed for the elevator.

"That was something," he remarked, struggling to sort out his muddled emotions as they stepped into the car.

She eyed him while they descended, letting the princess character drop away and becoming Lia in costume once more.

"From your tone I can't tell if that's good or bad."

"The kids really love you."

"Seeing their favorite princess come to life is a wonderful distraction for them."

"And you do this every week?"

Lia nodded. "I try to."

They reached the sidewalk and turned in the direction of the estate.

"Why?"

"You of all people should understand," she said, tugging at the fingers of one long yellow glove.

The movement snared Paul's attention and he noticed

an immediate and sharp uptick in his heartbeat as he watched her slide the material down her arm. The practiced move wasn't at all provocative or sexy, but made his breath quicken all the same.

"Why do you think I should understand?"

"Because of all the charity work your family does."

"Philanthropy and wealth usually go hand in hand."

"There's a difference between writing a big check and giving time and energy to a cause. Your family actively participates because that's what's rooted in their personal values."

Yet part of those values was defined by the idea that because of their good fortune the Wattses owed something to those less fortunate. Lia had no largesse, so why was she driven to help others? What compelled her to dress up and sing to children or to help Grady get better?

Despite all the facts he'd gleaned about her, today's hospital visit demonstrated how little he actually knew—or understood—about her.

"Thanks for coming along today," Lia said, rousing Paul from his thoughts.

He noticed that they were nearing the estate and found himself suddenly reluctant to part ways. "Do you want to come in for a drink?"

For a beat she stared at him as if debating how to respond, and then she shook her head. "I can't figure you out."

"The feeling is mutual."

"All week long you've been avoiding me. Now today

you come with me to the hospital and invite me for a drink. What's changed?"

What could he say? That he found her charming, her company invigorating? That avoiding her wasn't helping his peace of mind? He already knew their temperaments were completely different. Maybe if they spent more time together her eccentric ways and quirky beliefs would turn him off once and for all.

"Oh," she continued. "I'll bet you're scheming to get me drunk in the hopes I'll slip up and say something damning."

"Now who's the suspicious one," he retorted, wishing this was going more smoothly. As much as he didn't want to put his cards on the table, Paul realized he had to give her a peek at his hand if he hoped to entice her to extend their time together. "Maybe I enjoyed your company this afternoon and don't want it to end."

She blinked at him. "I'm sorry? Did I just hear you right? You enjoyed my company?"

"Do you want to join me for a drink or not?" he grumbled.

She tapped her finger against her lips, making a show of giving consideration to his invitation. "Well, since you asked so sweetly…sure. Let me change and check on Grady. It won't take me more than ten minutes."

"Need any help?" he asked, eyeing the gown's complicated lacings. "I've never undressed a princess before." The declaration came out of nowhere, surprising them both.

"If I thought you actually meant that," she said in a breathless rush, "I'd take you up on your offer."

Paul opened his mouth to either take back his remark or to double down, but before he decided which,
Lia threw up both hands and shook her head vigorously.

"No. Don't say anything more." She began retreating toward the house. "I'll be back in ten minutes. That
should give you plenty of time to figure out how to get
yourself out of trouble."

Lia's buoyant mood lingered as she walked along the
garden paths that led to the house. When she'd donned
the Belle costume, she'd never imagined such a magical
afternoon. She'd spent the last seven days anxious and
miserable over Paul's pronounced disapproval, unsure
how to cope with her body's irresistible response to his
physical appeal or to manage the push and pull of apprehension and lust that kept her off-balance.

Before today, if asked to describe Paul, Lia would
have used words like confident and authoritative. Yet at
the hospital today he'd shown her a different side, demonstrating he could be reflective and more openminded
than she'd imagined. This brief respite from his distrust
was a welcome change.

To her relief she encountered no one on the way to
her bedroom. Grady's door was closed, indicating he
was resting, no doubt worn out from his latest round of
physical therapy. Before leaving for the hospital, she'd
popped in to show off her costume. His delight at her
appearance had been nearly a match for the children.

Although Lia raced through her transformation she
took longer than ten minutes. Because the elaborate wig
and heavy gown left her feeling sweaty, she grabbed

a quick shower and hastily reapplied mascara and red lipstick because she wanted Paul to see her as attractive. Reluctant to keep him waiting too long, she drew her wet hair into a sleek topknot, and just before she headed out the door, swept powder over her nose, obliterating her freckles. She'd noticed how often Paul's gaze focused on the imperfection. No doubt he found them unsightly.

By the time she reached the carriage house, Lia was trembling with anticipation. How many nights had she gone to bed in Ava Watts's old bedroom only to find sleep elusive? Over and over she called herself a fool for letting the cybersecurity specialist get beneath her skin. While the man treated her like a thief out to steal the heirloom silver, she was tormented by fantasies of him making love to her with all the passion and intensity of a man who craved closeness and intimacy. And today, all he'd had to do was show her a little kindness and she was all in.

"Sorry I took so long," she said, covertly scanning his expression in search of reassurance. Was the man attracted to her or not? She couldn't tell. "The wig and dress left me feeling grimy so I showered."

He stepped close and lowered his head, breathing her in. "Damn, you smell good."

A lightning storm of awareness electrified Lia's whole body. She leaned back and peered up at his expression. He watched her through half-lidded eyes, predatory hunger smoldering in their green depths. Her pulse accelerated as his lips took on a sensual curve. The last time she'd seen that smile had been that afternoon at his beach house. Heat raced through her veins, bringing lethargy to her muscles and sparking hope. Emboldened, she reached out and cupped his cheek.

"You are attracted to me," she murmured, awestruck and filled with delight. "What happened last time was real."

"Very real." He wrapped his arm around her waist and pulled her close. "And something I promised myself would never happen again."

Crushing herself against his hard body, Lia breathed in his masculine scent. She wanted to burrow her hands beneath his clothes and slide her palms along his warm skin. "Why not?"

"You are pretending to be my cousin." His muscles tensed. "My first cousin."

"*Pretending* being the operative word." While Lia recognized that his argument held no water, she'd spent enough time in Charleston to understand that appearances were everything. "As long as we're careful and don't get caught…"

"Do you seriously think that's what I'm worried about?" He took her hands and eased them from his body, his grip gentle despite his frustrated tone. "Getting caught?"

"Isn't it?" She blinked at him in confusion as he set her free and took a half step back.

His bemused expression might have led her to ask more questions if her body wasn't aching with the sharpest longing. Day and night, she'd tormented herself with revisiting that kiss at his beach house, taking things past the moment when he'd stopped. She'd imagined a hundred variations. Them going inside and making love in his bed. Him drawing her into the hot tub and making her come while she floated on a raft of bubbles. Her dropping to her knees to pleasure him in full sight of the beach while he held tight to the deck railing and shouted his pleasure.

"Look, if you're worried that I might fall for you..." She shook her head, hoping she could be convincing. "Don't. I find you attractive. It's just sex."

From the first stirring of physical attraction, she'd accepted that they had no future. Even before she started posing as his first cousin, he'd regarded her with suspicion and she doubted he'd ever fully trust her. In so many ways, from their upbringings to their temperaments, they were completely incompatible. Never in her wildest daydreams could she imagine he'd walk into a public venue and be proud to call her his date much less his girlfriend.

But their chemistry couldn't be denied. That left sex. Great sex. Because after being kissed by Paul Watts, Lia knew the guy would be fantastic in bed. She shivered in anticipation of his strong hands running over her naked body. Just imagining how he would slide his finger through the slippery wetness between her thighs caused her body to clench in pleasure.

"Just sex," he echoed, murmuring the two words in a contemplative tone. "And in a week you'll be gone."

While her heart bucked painfully in her chest, Lia nodded. "That's the plan."

"Nobody could possibly fall for someone that fast." He raked her expression with hard green eyes. "I mean it's only a week."

"Absolutely." Damn the man could talk, but she was starting to see a glimmer of hope. "That's not enough time to get attached."

Lia wasn't sure which of them moved first, but the next thing she knew, he'd cupped the back of her neck in his hand and her fingers had tunneled into his hair. Then they were lip-locked and moaning beneath the onslaught of desire and need.

"That's more like it," Lia murmured a long while later after he released her lips and trailed kisses down her throat. "Damn, you are good at that."

"At what?"

He brought his teeth together on the place where her neck and shoulder joined. Pleasure shot through her at the tantalizing pain of his bite. She groaned as his tongue flicked over the spot, soothing the sting. Desire tore through her. Lia couldn't recall ever feeling so alive or invigorated.

"Kissing," she said. "I thought maybe you were too focused on chasing bad guys to ever make time for a love life."

"So you thought I was inexperienced when it came to women?"

He didn't wait for her to reply before seizing her mouth for another hard, demanding kiss that left her weak-kneed and flushed from head to toe. His fingers dug into her hip as she rocked into him, before he sent his palm coasting downward over her butt. When he lifted her against his growing erection, Lia panted in frustration at the pressure building in her.

His lips moved over the shell of her ear, awakening a

million goose bumps. Adrift in pleasure, she didn't expect the sharp nip on her earlobe or the way fireworks detonated in her loins, setting her on fire.

"Have you thought about us together?" he asked, his voice a low purr that sent a riot of tingles along her nerves.

She nodded.

"Is this how it went?"

"Sometimes." She could scarcely speak above a whisper.

"Have you imagined me bending you over and taking you from behind."

The image was only one of a hundred different scenarios she'd toyed with. "Yes."

For a microsecond his whole body went perfectly still. "My mouth between your thighs, driving you crazy?"

"Yes." This time she moaned the word.

His teeth raked down her neck. "I think about your mouth on me."

"Yes," she pleaded. "Oh, yes."

"Wicked girl." He sounded so pleased by her response.

She sighed in relief when his hand slid between her thighs, fingers applying the perfect pressure over the spot where she ached. While she rocked against his palm, his tongue plunged into her mouth over and over. Mindless, her arousal gaining intensity, she rubbed her clit against his hand. With the barrier of her clothes between them, equal parts frustration and delight prompted the incoherent sounds coming from her throat. At last she could take it no more.

"Damn it, Paul," she panted, her desperation giving her voice a shrill edge.

He lifted his head and regarded her from beneath his thick dark lashes. "What?"

Even as she struggled to find the words to tell him what she wanted, he sent his fingers skimming beneath the waistband of her yoga pants and followed the neat landing strip to where she burned. The pleasure was so overwhelming that she huffed out a laugh to relieve some of the strain of keeping her delight bottled up.

"I was just thinking that I should've waxed an arrow to point the way for you."

It was the first thing that popped into her head and one corner of his lips kicked up in a mocking salute.

"Baby, I know exactly where I'm going." Even before he finished speaking, he stroked through her hot core.

The move left her just enough breath for an awe-struck curse. "Damn."

"You're incredible," he murmured, raking his teeth over her lower lip. "I can't believe how wet you are. That's so damn sexy."

He stroked his fingers through her slippery wetness, whispering his admiration, letting her know how much he appreciated her. Moaning, she shifted her hips, wanting his fingers inside her. The building pressure was almost too much to bear.

"Please," she panted, gathering a handful of his silky blond hair and tugging. "Make me come."

"My pleasure."

She shuddered in anticipation as he dropped to his knees and dragged her yoga pants and panties down her thighs. A moment later he leaned forward and drew his tongue along the seam that hid her sex from him. Lia's muscles failed her and she would've collapsed without his supportive grip.

"Hold on," he warned, a smile in his voice as his tongue speared into the heart of her.

An old commercial played through her head as Paul drove her excitement still higher. *How many licks does it take to get Lia off? One. Two. Three.* Just that fast she found herself coming. The speed and intensity of her climax blew her mind.

"Paul…" She threw her head back and welcomed the orgasm that blasted through her. Curses fell from her lips at the intensity of the pleasure.

"Wow," he murmured, trailing kisses across her abdomen as her muscles quaked with aftershocks. "You are a firecracker."

Not surprising since she'd had a week of foreplay to prime the pump. To her dismay, he reached down and slid her pants back into place before getting to his feet.

"Are we done?"

He raised his eyebrows at her scandalized tone, but long lashes hid the expression in his gaze. The roughness in his voice, however, gave him away as he breathed, "I hope not."

"Then kiss me again and let's take this thing horizontal."

He put his arm around her, hand sliding to cup her butt while he rubbed his erection against her hip. She savored the hard length of him poking at her and shimmied to add even more friction. The taste of herself on his lips made her eager to have her way with him in turn. Even though she hadn't yet gotten her hands on the bulge behind his zipper, she could tell he was well built.

A staccato horn beeped nearby as someone locked a car. At the interruption of their thoroughly hot and promising embrace, Paul tore his mouth from hers. Female voices intruded on the sensual fog Lia had gotten caught up in. Paul's hands fell away from her body as he abruptly stepped back. His physical withdrawal left her shivering as if doused with cold water. Her eyes flew open in time to see shutters slam down over his expression. Only his heightened color and his unwillingness to look at her hinted at the passion he'd recently demonstrated.

A second later a knock sounded on the carriage house door and Lia almost whimpered in disappointment as she recognized Poppy's voice.

"Hey, Paul, are you there?"

A muscle jumped in his jaw as he shot a hard look at the door. "I have to answer that."

"Of course." She drew in a shaky breath as his gaze raked over her. Feeling exposed and raw in the aftermath of such all-consuming desire, Lia craved some privacy to recover her wits before facing the twins. "Can I borrow your bathroom?"

"In there." He pointed down the hallway and headed for the front door.

To her dismay, as soon as she met her gaze in the mirror, Lia found herself blinking back a rush of unexpected tears. She braced her hands on the sink and rode the wave of emotions until her breath steadied and she could smile without grimacing.

Although he'd been clear that lying to his family bothered him, Lia recognized that sneaking around added spice to their encounters. And she couldn't imagine Paul being susceptible to such a thing—doubtless he'd never allowed himself to be in a situation like theirs before. And he wasn't the only one.

During her years on the road, she'd had many men look at her lifestyle and view her as a short-term thing. Unlike her mother, who took frequent lovers, Lia needed some sort of a connection and rarely found it. What she'd just had with Paul was worth more than all her experiences combined and it left her wondering—if she'd found this before, would she have stayed put?

Lia loved her life on the road. Traveling around the country satisfied her restless nature and offered her the opportunity to experience places that people often missed because they either flew to their destinations or only visited tourist locations.

Her time stranded in Charleston had given Lia an opportunity to think about what she wanted for the future. Was she going to roam aimlessly for the rest of her life or should she put down roots somewhere? And what was her criteria for staying? She'd found much to like in Charleston, but did it feel like home? Was she drawn to the place or the people or both? Lia's inability to answer told her to move on.

She cracked the door to hear the conversation just

in time to recall that she'd committed to spending the afternoon with the twins.

"She's going to tell our fortunes," Poppy was saying to Paul, referring to Lia's promise to bring out her tarot deck and read for them. "You have to come and have your cards read, too."

"It's all foolishness," Paul said, sounding exasperated.

"Come on," Dallas insisted. "I'm trying out some new recipes for Zoe and Ryan's wedding and there will be cocktails. It'll be fun."

"Please," Poppy wheedled. "You never hang out with us anymore."

"Fine. I'll be there."

"Awesome," Dallas said. "Half an hour."

"And leave your skepticism at the door," Poppy said. "The universe might have an important message for you."

Once Paul had ushered out his cousins and shut the door, Lia returned to the great room, a brave smile plastered on her face to hide her disappointment at the change in plans.

"She's right," Lia said, striding toward him. From his closed expression and rigid posture, she guessed the intimacy they'd shared five minutes earlier had been shattered by the twins' visit. "You should come with an open mind. The cards have a way of getting to the truth."

Paul stood with his hand on the doorknob and gazed down his nose at her. "Fortune-telling is all just educated guesses and made-up stuff."

"It can be," Lia agreed, thinking their differences couldn't be any clearer. "But sometimes if you open your heart, the answers will shine like the midday sun."

"Except I don't ask those sorts of questions."

Questions that might encourage him to lead with his heart and not his head. Lia knew nothing she could say would convince him otherwise so she pushed down her disappointment and vowed to only ask of him what she knew he could give.

Six

From Paul's perch on a barstool at the breakfast bar in the caretaker house kitchen, he could observe the shenanigans playing out at the dining room table without appearing to be engaged. He was working his way through the second of the three cocktails Dallas had prepared for them to taste. She'd dubbed this one Love Potion, and with two shots of vodka and one of bourbon mixed with both cranberry and cherry juice, it packed a punch.

Despite being identical twins, with their mother's blond hair and blue eyes, Dallas and Poppy had vastly distinct styles and temperaments. The oldest by ten minutes, Dallas had the Watts family head for business and more than her fair share of ambition. Since graduating college, she'd worked for some of the best restaurants in

Charleston with the goal of opening her own place and currently worked as a private chef and caterer.

By contrast, Poppy was a stylist at a high-end salon in downtown Charleston and an active beauty blogger. She was free-spirited and headstrong, with striking pink hair and boundless energy, and whenever her family questioned her about doing something more serious than cutting hair, her quick answer was always a flippant one.

"Hey, Paul," Poppy called, breaking into his musings. "It's your turn."

He blinked several times to reorient his thoughts and noticed that he was the center of attention. "I'm not interested." He hoped his resolute tone would dissuade them from pestering him further, but their eager gazes remained fixed on him.

"Oh come on, we've both done it." Dallas shot Lia a look. "What are you afraid of?"

"Besides," Poppy chimed in. "It's not fair that you've heard all our dark secrets without spilling a few of your own."

"I don't..." Paul trailed off. He'd been about to deny having any dark secrets, but then realized since Lia had arrived, he had more each day. "You know this isn't my cup of tea."

"Ladies, leave him alone," Lia said, no disappointment or censure in her unruffled manner. She gathered up the cards from Poppy's reading and returned them to the stack.

"Obviously he's afraid to face the truth," Dallas said, displaying relentless determination.

For the last hour, while Lia had made credible-sounding

predictions for the twins, Paul had grown increasingly skeptical of her glib performance. While her expertise had appeared genuine enough to thoroughly engage his cousins, in Paul's opinion the concept of being able to predict the future based on the turn of a card was nothing but nonsense. Still, as much as he'd wanted to scoff several times over the past hour, he'd held his tongue because Dallas and Poppy were thoroughly enjoying the experience. Or at least they were making a show of doing so. Some of Lia's prognostications had rattled both girls, although they'd laughed and sipped their drinks to cover it up.

"There's no truth I'm afraid to face," Paul declared, his gaze clashing with both his cousins' even as Lia kept her focus on the tarot deck. He was mesmerized by her small hands as she shuffled the deck to clear the energy. Why didn't she chime in? Surely, she was dying to feed him a load of rubbish to get a rise out of him. "I just see all of this as a huge waste of time."

"Since when is having fun a waste of time?" Poppy asked.

"When it comes to Paul," Dallas piped up, "since always."

"Come on, Paul." Poppy got up from where she was sitting across from Lia and gestured for him to replace her. "What does it hurt to have Lia read for you?"

Seeing the two women weren't going to let him escape without taking a turn in the hot seat as Lia had mockingly called it, Paul finished the Love Potion cocktail and made his way to the chair Poppy had vacated. Lia's hazel eyes gleamed as she pushed the cards across the table toward him. From the first two rounds, he knew she wanted him to shuffle the cards. She explained that this would let the cards absorb his energy.

"While you shuffle, think about something you want to ask the cards about." Lia had issued this instruction with both the earlier readings.

"Really," he insisted. "There's nothing."

Lia nodded. "Then just let your mind drift."

Paul handled the cards indifferently, demonstrating that he viewed the whole activity as a grand waste of time, yet while he shuffled the deck, mixing them thoroughly the way he'd watched his cousins do, he found himself besieged by memories of those delicious minutes with Lia in his carriage house. The taste of her. The way she'd given herself over to him. His name on her lips as she'd come.

His body tightened at the vivid images and he shifted uncomfortably on the chair before setting the cards on the silk cloth she'd spread on the dining table. "You know I don't buy into any of this stuff," he muttered with barely restrained impatience.

"You don't believe and that's okay." Lia had been staring at the cards in his hands, but now she lifted her gaze to meet his. The impact made his heart stumble. "But you never know. You might hear something interesting."

A tiny ember of curiosity flared as he wondered what she might tell him. He suspected it would give him insight into her motives. No doubt she'd try to guide him into some sort of behavior the way she had his cousins, telling Dallas that she'd soon be confronted with a difficult decision involving two men in her life and

Poppy that she would undergo a transformative period that would shake up her status quo and possibly harm those around her.

Both of these vague but somewhat ominous predictions had puzzled the twins, but they'd eagerly embraced the readings as if they were a road map to their futures.

"Go ahead and cut the cards," Lia instructed. "Make three piles just like your cousins did."

Paul did as she told him and made three similarly sized piles. The ritual of handling the tarot cards had given the process a solemnity that made a strong impression on his cousins.

"Now pick one pile," Lia said.

His immediate instinct was to point to the one in the center, but as his finger was moving to indicate that stack, his gaze veered away.

"This one," he said, indicating the one to the right, unable to explain why he'd changed course.

With a reverent nod, Lia gathered up the deck, placing the stack he had chosen on the top. Then she began to lay the cards out in a particular order facedown the way she had with his cousins. She'd called it a Celtic Cross and remarked that the layout was one of the most traditional.

"Ready?" she asked.

"Yes." He growled the word from between clenched teeth as he noticed a trace of excitement mingling with anxiety bubbling in his gut. Refusing to fall for Lia's theatrics, he ruthlessly tamped down the emotions.

As if drawn to the drama unfolding at the dining room table, his cousins raced over and took the empty seats on either side of him. Eyes bright with curious intensity, they leaned forward, their full plates and re-filled crystal tumblers forgotten.

"We'll start with these two in the center," Lia in-toned, indicating the crossed cards.

She pulled the bottom one out first and flipped it over, revealing an old man with a long gray beard and bowed back. He carried a lantern and leaned on a walk-ing stick. The character reminded Paul of Gandalf the Grey from *The Lord of the Rings* trilogy.

"This is the Hermit reversed," Lia said. "It indicates what's currently influencing you. It's crossed by..." A dramatic pause followed as she turned over the next card. "The Fool. It is the first card of the Major Arcana and indicates the beginnings of a journey. The Fool can represent following your instincts despite what might seem the more sensible practice." Lia touched the Her-mit card. "As you can see the Hermit is upside down. This indicates that your time of isolation is over. You are ready to rejoin your community."

Paul glanced from Lia to Poppy to Dallas and back to Lia as he absorbed her words. All three women were completely engrossed and he had to resist the urge to snort derisively. Let them have their fun. Nothing Lia said so far pertained to him. He didn't isolate himself. He worked long hours to make sure his clients' data was safe. As for starting a journey...he had no plans to travel anywhere.

Lia flipped over the card below the first two. "This position is the basis of the situation."

"That doesn't look like a very happy scene," Dallas said.

Paul peered at the image on the card and frowned. Two people slogging through the snow, their backs hunched, looking very much as if they were lost and having a very difficult time. Above them was a glowing church window with five circles.

"Many interpret the Five of Pentacles as a dire financial situation," Lia said. "But I often read it as someone who either can't see a helping hand being extended to them or is unable to accept the aid being offered."

As expected, none of this made any sense. Paul forced down his impatience. He wasn't in a situation where he had need of anyone's assistance. With the exception of Lia's appearance in their lives, everything in Paul's orbit ran as smooth as clockwork.

"What's in Paul's past?" Poppy asked, pointing to the card in the nine o'clock position.

Lia turned it over. "The Three of Wands, indicating someone who has achieved much and is now satisfied with all they've done." She lifted her gaze from the cards and regarded Paul. "I think that sums up your past perfectly. You've spent a lot of time working hard on your business and now you get to look forward to what's next. The position above is possible outcome." She flipped the card over.

"Whoa," Dallas murmured. "That's grim."

The card showed a woman standing blindfolded and bound in front of a semicircle of swords. The bleakness of the image made him suddenly glad that it wasn't a definite outcome. Even as that thought crossed his mind, he rejected it. This was nothing more than a foolish pastime. None of this meant anything.

"This is a potential outcome," Lia pointed out.

Poppy worried her lower lip. "It doesn't seem like Paul is destined for a happy ending."

"The key to this card is the blindfold," Lia said. "It symbolizes confusion and isolation. But notice that while her arms are bound, her legs are free. She could walk away from this dangerous situation at any point. Instead, she's choosing to stay where she is." Lia moved on. "This next position is near future. It shows some situation that you will soon have to face, but not with the same certainty as the outcome. However, it can influence how things turn out."

As she finished speaking, she flipped the card over and Paul's heart stopped dead at the sight of the two naked people on the card with the sun shining down and an angel hovering around them.

Poppy squealed with delight. "The Lovers."

"Well, well, well," Dallas said. "Paul, what aren't you telling us?"

To his dismay, he felt a rush of heat beneath his skin. It couldn't be possible. Lia must have managed some trick with the deck. There was no other explanation for why this card had shown up in this position after what had almost happened between them.

After what he wanted to happen between them.

"Looks like I'm going to get lucky," he remarked, retreating into humor to cover his discomfort.

"Good for you," Poppy said, making it sound like he'd been neglecting his sex life.

Dallas nodded her agreement. "Maybe you'll meet someone at Ryan's wedding who you'll click with."

Paul was standing up for his best friend at a small, private wedding in a few days. The speed with which Ryan had fallen for Zoe continued to bemuse Paul, but he had no hesitations about the two being perfect for each other.

"Unlikely," Paul said, "since I know everyone who'll be there." Yet, even as he spoke Paul couldn't stop himself from glancing Lia's way. In truth, he'd already met someone who intrigued him.

"The Lovers card doesn't always mean the obvious," Lia said, injecting a calm note in the conversation. "In some instances it can be a choice between two things he loves."

"Do you have two things you love, Paul?" Dallas asked.

"The only thing he loves is working," Poppy put in.

He gave each of them a sour look before settling a heavy-lidded gaze on Lia. Since starting the reading, she'd mostly been actively avoiding looking his way, preferring to concentrate on the cards before her, but as soon as the Lovers card had appeared, a trace of color bloomed in her cheeks as if she, too, was thinking about what had happened between them.

"The card at the bottom of the staff indicates self," Lia said, resuming the reading. "The attitude you are contributing to the situation." She flipped the card over exposing a king sitting on a throne with a sword. "Yes," she murmured, "this makes sense. The King represents authority, power and judgment. He likes to rule the world with his keen mind and forceful personality."

"That sounds exactly like you," Dallas said.

"Totally," her sister echoed.

"This next card is your environment." Lia flipped the card over. The Two of Cups.

"I had that one, as well," Dallas said. "You said it stood for romance. Look, it's right next to the Lovers." She pointed to the proximity of the two cards. "It seems like Paul may be headed straight for love."

"What?" Paul muttered, unable to contain his displeasure. "Are you an expert now?"

While Dallas grinned at him in cheeky confidence, Lia shook her head.

"Or it could just mean that he's torn between two things that are really important to him," she said. "Perhaps he needs to balance his time better between family and his love for chasing criminals."

Her interpretation sounded so reasonable, yet all this talk about romance, love and sex was making him itchy.

"What about the last two cards?" he demanded, impatient to have the whole reading done.

"This position is your hopes and fears." Lia pointed to the second-to-the-last position, and then shifted her finger to indicate the one above it. "And this is your final outcome."

"So what do they say?" Poppy asked, her blue eyes dancing with anticipation.

Lia turned the first card over. From Paul's vantage point, the image appeared to be a man dancing on top of a log, but he realized that he was looking at the card upside down and that the man was actually hanging by his feet.

"That doesn't look good," he said.

"It's not as bad as it looks," Lia countered. "The Hanged Man symbolizes peace and understanding. However, he believes the only way to maintain this state is by withdrawing from society. He's similar to the Hermit. He's serene because he's locked up his emotions for years."

"And the last one?" Paul demanded, ready to be done.

Lia flipped over the final card to reveal a single chalice, balanced on a palm and suspended over the ocean. "The Ace of Cups indicates a time of happiness and love. A gift of joy."

"So," Dallas began, "if I'm hearing this correctly, Paul has been alone too long and he's going to start a new relationship, but he's going to fight his feelings because he's locked up his emotions for so long that he's afraid of them, but in the end it's all going to work out and he'll be very happy."

While Dallas summarized the reading and Poppy nodded her agreement, Lia studied the cards. A frown line appeared between her brows. Had Lia twisted the reading to suit her needs in the hopes that he would believe himself falling for her? If so, she didn't look as pleased as Paul would've expected, given the strong romantic overtones of the cards.

Poppy turned her bright gaze on him. "I can't wait to meet the lucky woman."

Paul very deliberately kept his attention from straying to Lia as he replied, "This isn't a great time for me to focus on my personal life."

Dallas chuckled. "I like the way you believe you'll have a choice." She indicated the cards. "Looks to me like your future is clear. There's romance on your horizon and it's going to change everything."

As Dallas summed up her take on Paul's tarot spread, Lia gathered up the cards and put them away. While she'd been reading for the twins, he'd worn an indulgent half smile. Now, however, he'd retreated behind an impassive expression and only the slight dip in his eyebrows indicated that he was disgruntled.

Either the twins were accustomed to ignoring their cousin's bouts of irritation or they didn't notice that he was troubled. For Lia, Paul's displeasure was palpable. She tried shooting him a reassuring smile, but all that produced was a narrowing of his eyes.

It seemed impossible that she could be falling for someone as serious-minded as Paul Watts. Yet after what had happened between them in the carriage house, Lia recognized that without their growing emotional connection, the earth-shattering orgasm he'd given her wouldn't have been possible. She'd never known that sort of all-consuming passion.

In some ways it terrified her. She was accustomed to being able to pick up and go whenever the mood hit her. She didn't have any emotional ties that limited her freedom. Traveling like a leaf on the wind of her whims was how she'd grown up. Her mother's idea of a perfect lifestyle seemed perfectly rational to Lia given what had happened to Jen Marsh.

No one got close when you moved all the time.

No attachments meant no heartbreak. Or that was how it was supposed to work.

"What did you think of your first tarot reading?" Lia asked as they strolled along that path that led away from the caretaker's house.

"You know I don't believe in any of that stuff."

"I get it." Lia knew his skepticism would continue to come between them if she reacted defensively. "You're a logical guy. It's not really your thing."

"All that business about a future romance and having to choose between two things that I love," Paul continued, his tone thoughtful rather than dismissive.

As she struggled to make sense of what was bothering him, Lia realized that Paul had seen enough truth in the reading to be unsettled by it. How was that possible? He was too much of a realist to do anything but reject all he'd seen and heard today.

"If you aren't ready for love then that's not likely to happen for you," she reassured him, despite having seen the opposite happen when the cards predicted romance. But if anyone could avoid his emotions or anything that distracted him from business, it was Paul. "Maybe the universe is just nudging you to work less and spend more quality time with family and friends." From the way he scowled at her, Lia should've kept the advice to herself. Awash in sudden frustration, she threw up her hands. "Look. What do I know? It's your life."

They walked in tense silence until the path was joined by one that stretched between the house and driveway. Lia started to turn away, but Paul touched his fingertips to her arm, stopping her.

"I know it's last-minute, but I was wondering if you'd like to come with me to Ryan and Zoe's wedding on Saturday."

Lia laid her fist over her rapidly thumping heart. "I thought you wanted me to keep a low profile."

"It's a small gathering of my close friends. None of them will spread gossip around Charleston about you."

His declaration struck her as naive and shortsighted.

"Given how your cousins reacted to the tarot card reading," she said, "there's more interest in your love life than you realize."

"If anyone asks, we'll just say you're a family friend in town for a short visit."

Lia studied his impassive expression, knowing she shouldn't read too much into his offer. Her instincts warned her that spending more time with Paul was a mistake, but the temptation was so strong.

"Let me guess," she said, concealing her jumbled emotions behind mockery. "You were so busy catching bad guys that you forgot to invite anyone and you don't want to go to the wedding alone."

His crushing glare confirmed her hypothesis, but his fingers skimmed down her arm and trailed over the back of her hand. The urge to drag him back to the carriage house and finish what they'd started made her shiver.

"Why do you have to make everything so difficult?"

he demanded, his impatient tone at odds with the fire dancing in his eyes.

"Funny," she snorted. "I was thinking the same thing about you."

The air around them sizzled as Lia turned her hand and placed her palm against Paul's. She barely bit back a groan as he intertwined their fingers. For several silent seconds they stared at each other until Lia's phone chimed, indicating she'd received a text. It took a supreme effort of will to break eye contact with Paul. Glancing down at the screen, she noted that Ethan had sent her a message.

"Something wrong?" Paul quizzed.

"Ethan was going to give me a ride to my camper so I could pick up a costume, and then we were going to go truck shopping, but he has to go into a late meeting so he can't make it." Lia considered her options as she continued, "The nurses are throwing a birthday party for one of the children at the hospital on Saturday and I promised to surprise her with a visit from Elsa."

"I can take you."

"You don't have to do that," she murmured, turning him down despite the craving to spend more time in his company. "Ethan—"

"Forget about Ethan."

His firm command sent a ripple of pleasure cascading through her body. Before meeting Paul, she never imagined herself attracted to someone so authoritative and formidable. He was as set in his ways as a granite boulder while she glided past, a butterfly borne on the winds of chance. The lack of compatibility in their natures offered no reason why they should have the slightest hint of chemistry, yet the pull between them couldn't be denied.

"I don't want to bother you," she protested.

"It's too late for that," he growled, the sound sinking into her bones, turning them to mush. "Text Ethan and tell him I'll take care of you."

Lia shivered at his words, every cell in her body sparkling with delight. "Really, it's okay. I can ask one of the twins…"

"Is there a reason why you suddenly want to be rid of me?"

"I don't want to be rid of you," she retorted in exasperation.

Paul frowned. "Is there a reason why you prefer going out with Ethan over me?"

"It's not that I prefer Ethan's company."

"Then what is it?" Paul persisted.

"The thing is, I think you view me as a tad eccentric—"

"A tad," he agreed, a teasing note in his voice.

Despite his attempt at levity, she remained earnest. "It's just that taking you to where I live is intimate."

All emotion vanished from his expression. "More intimate than what we did earlier?"

"For me, yes. Misty is my safe place. No matter what else changes in my life, she's a constant, my refuge." And being away from the camper, disconnected from the nomadic lifestyle for so many months, had caused a shift in her identity that left her feeling vulnerable and a bit lost.

"And I'm not welcome in your safe place."

"No, I mean…" She scrambled to explain without causing further damage to their fragile rapport.

"But Ethan is?"

"It's different with him," Lia said.

"Different how?"

"We're friends."

"Friends." His jaw worked as if he was grinding the word to dust.

"What I'm trying to say is that I've known him for months and we've talked about a lot of things."

"Are these the sorts of things you don't feel comfortable sharing with me?"

Lia thought about the differences between the two men. Ethan was more like a brother who accepted her oddities. Paul was a shining beacon of all things correct, perfect and gorgeous. From the start he'd been vocal about all her flaws and limitations. Lately she'd glimpsed grudging admiration for how she'd helped his grandfather. At the same time, Lia suspected if Paul hadn't been so suspicious of her from the start, she might never have registered on his radar.

"Ethan sees me. He accepts who I am."

"And you don't think I do?"

When his fingers tightened, Lia realized they were still holding hands. Suddenly aware that they could be discovered by one of his family at any second, Lia tried to tug free.

"You have a bad opinion of me," he declared, looking stunned.

"I don't," she countered.

"On the other hand, you have a high opinion of Ethan."

"Look." Deciding it was fruitless to dance around the truth any longer, Lia stripped all finesse out of her justification. "Ethan isn't likely to judge me for living in a camper."

"But you think I would." Paul released her hand and stepped back. "Let me point out that you are the one jumping to conclusions about me. Which is ironic, considering I spent the last hour watching you read tarot cards and didn't utter a single disparaging remark."

"You're right. I… I'm…"

"Sorry?" He crossed his arms over his chest. "You should be. I've been pretty openminded about all the alternative treatments you've used on Grady. Meditation. Sound baths. Aromatherapy. I've never met anyone who believes in the sorts of things you do, but I've never tried to interfere with anything you've suggested."

"You're right," she repeated. Lia bowed her head and accepted the scolding. "I'm not being fair to you. I know the things I'm into are completely foreign to you and you've been great about all the weirdness." She paused and looked into his eyes, then said, "If you're still willing to take me to pick up the Elsa costume, I'm happy to go for the ride."

"Afterward we'll go truck shopping," he declared, his tone brooking no further discussion. "And then I'll take you to dinner."

"That would be very nice," she said in a small voice, offering him a tentative smile. "Give me ten minutes to put the deck back in my room and get my purse."

He nodded in satisfaction, but his expression had yet to relax. "I'll meet you by the driveway."

Seven

While Paul waited for Lia, he paced from his SUV to the edge of the driveway and back, made restless by his heightened emotional state. Gone were the days when he could summon icy calm and a clear head at will. Just being near Lia disrupted the status quo. The factual logic that had served him all his life was being defeated by things he couldn't see, touch or prove existed. He was actually buying into all her metaphysical nonsense. His tarot reading had struck far too close to home. He'd like to put it down to sleight-of-hand card tricks and guesswork, but she hadn't touched the tarot deck after he'd handled it.

He'd always viewed his suspicious nature as a fundamental part of him like his height and eye color. Innate and something he couldn't change even if he wanted to.

He could see how his skepticism created distance from others, but he'd accepted this as a matter of course. He had faith in those who were important to him. His family. Close friends. The rest of the world could go to hell.

But lately he was growing increasingly aware of how his distrust impacted Lia. She lacked the sort of armor those he usually dealt with wore. Her openness and upbeat take on the world displayed vulnerability that charmed everyone she met.

Which made her resistance to letting him see her camper all the more striking.

She didn't trust him.

The revelation stung.

Worse was her blind faith in Ethan. Had she forgotten which brother had landed her in their current predicament? Ethan, not Paul, had been the one who'd perpetuated Grady's incorrect belief that Lia was his long-lost granddaughter. More than any other member of the Watts family, Ethan was the one she should be most wary of.

"Ready?"

Paul had been so lost in thought that he hadn't noticed Lia's approach. She'd done more than grab her purse at the house. While he'd wrestled with his demons, she'd changed into a loose-fitting black-and-white-striped T-shirt dress and white sneakers. With her hair in a loose topknot and dark glasses hiding her eyes, she gave off a cool, casual vibe at complete odds with the turmoil raging in him.

Longing rippled through him. He itched to reach across the distance separating them and haul her into his arms. Instead, stunned by the willpower it took to keep his hands off her, he gripped the passenger-side door handle as if it was a lifeline and gestured her into the SUV. No matter how temptation swelled in him, this wasn't the time or place to cross that line. Why was it so hard to do the right thing around her?

Forty minutes later, Paul drove through the security gate of a boat and RV storage lot and stopped his SUV beside a small vintage trailer painted white and mint green. From Lia's doting expression, he gathered this must be the famous Misty.

"It won't take me but a second to grab the costume," Lia said, her hand on the door handle. "Do you want to wait here?"

After their earlier quarrel, he intended to prove that he wasn't the judgmental jerk she'd branded him. "No." And then hearing how abrupt that sounded, he added in a more conciliatory tone, "I'd like to see what she looks like inside." He'd picked up Lia's habit of referring to the vintage camper by the feminine pronoun.

"Okay." She drew the word out as she exited the SUV.

Paul noted the matching mint-colored curtains framing the windows as Lia unlocked the camper and stepped inside. He followed her in, surprised that the ceiling height accommodated his six-foot-one-inch frame without him having to stoop.

"This is tiny," he declared, at once shocked by the camper's limited footprint and impressed by how Lia had made efficient use of every inch of it. "How do you live in such a small space?"

"Simply." She flashed him a wry grin and gestured at the boxes piled up in the sitting area toward the back. "It's not usually this cluttered. Normally I store all the costumes in my truck."

"Do you like living with so little?" Paul asked, shifting uneasily in the narrow aisle between closet and kitchen. He became all too aware of the inviting sleeping nook behind him with its extravagance of soft pillows.

"I find it calming." She gave him a quick tour, narrating the camper's history while assessing his reaction the whole time. "What do you think?"

"It's cozy," he ventured, glancing around. "And it suits you."

Into less than one hundred and fifty square feet, she'd fit a kitchen and bathroom, full-size bed, dinette and a decent-sized closet. Vintage pastel fabrics softened the white walls, tin-tile ceiling and wood-look vinyl flooring. The appliances were the same mint green as the exterior and appeared original to the 1960s' vibe.

"Thank you."

"For what?"

"Being openminded." Her infectious smile bloomed for the first time since Dallas had interrupted them at the carriage house. "You know, we aren't likely to get interrupted anytime soon." While he processed what she'd said, she blew out an exasperated breath. "Are you just going to stare at me?" Giving his shirt a sassy tug, she finished, "Or are you going to take me in your arms and rock my world?"

Relief flooded him. They were going to be okay. Paul wrapped his arm around her waist and hauled her up against him. The breath swept out of her in a soft, satisfying huff. He expected her to get all clingy and press herself against him, but instead she wrapped her arms around his waist and rested her cheek on his chest.

"What are you doing?" Paul asked.

She flexed her arm muscles, embracing him more snugly. "Giving you a hug."

"Why?"

"I want you to know that I like you." Without lifting her cheek from the front of his shirt, she canted her head and gazed up at him. "Before you kiss me. Before I go all weak-kneed and gooey inside. I want you to know I like you. You. Not your money. Or the power your family wields in this town. I'm a simple girl with simple needs. One of them being a gorgeous, sexy man who makes love to her as if she's the most desirable woman he's ever known."

It was both a request and a plea for him to treat her well. But her declaration tempered Paul's all-consuming drive to possess her. He eased his grip, second-guessing everything.

"Why is that important before I kiss you?"

"I don't think this time we'll be able to stop there," she said. "And after whatever happens you'll be even less willing to trust me."

"It's not that I don't trust you…" It was more that he didn't trust himself around her. The feelings she aroused messed with his head.

"You trust that I'm good for your grandfather. But I don't think you'll ever trust that I could be good for you."

With his gaze locked on her lips, he rasped, "That's not true."

But he recognized the reason for her apprehension. He approached decisions with logic; she believed a deck of cards could predict what was to come. She took leaps of faith with little regard for her own safety. He rarely made a move without knowing in advance what the outcome would be. Yet at the moment he felt driven beyond wisdom and sense by his need for her.

"You won't believe that I don't want anything from you," she persisted. "Even when nothing I've done gives you any reason to suspect me."

It should've bothered him that she had him all figured out. Well, maybe not all figured out. But her grasp on what made him tick surpassed what he understood about her.

"I don't have all the answers," he admitted. "You're not like anyone I've ever known before and frankly, you scare the hell out of me."

Her eyes widened. "I don't see how."

"You've brought magic into my life." He braced his hip against her kitchen counter as his admission caused something inside him to snap. Light-headed and reeling, he closed his eyes.

"You don't believe in magic," she murmured.

"I believe in you."

He dropped his head and let his breath flow over her lips before easing forward to taste her. Anticipating a powerful jolt of desire, he was unprepared for the way his entire body lit up like he'd backed into a high-voltage generator marked *Danger*.

Drinking deep of her sweet, sinful mouth, Paul savored a kiss that reminded him of a quality bourbon, warm and complex. Heat spiraled through his veins. Her moan gave him the signal to take the kiss deeper. Lost in the liquid slide of their dancing tongues, Paul sucked on her lower lip and smiled as an eager groan broke from her throat. Their teeth clicked and he slanted his head to adjust the angle of the kiss so he could continue to devour her unhindered.

Lia's questing fingers dove beneath his shirt and an electrical storm flashed behind his closed eyes. He crackled with wild thrumming energy.

He came up for air long enough to whisper, "This is going to complicate things."

"Oh." The anguish in her murmur made him hate that he'd voiced his concerns. But then she kept going and it was her throaty yes that sealed both their fates.

He breathed in her laughter, capturing it in his lungs before crushing his mouth to hers. A needy whimper broke from her as she ground herself against him, her movement becoming more frantic by the second. She rocked her hips, as if she'd given herself over to what her body needed and to hell with pride or consequences.

Paul couldn't get enough of this woman. The chemistry between them was born of Lia's romantic optimism and his surrender to everything caring and earnest about her. Even knowing this stolen moment couldn't last and despite recognizing her sweetness might shatter his defenses and leave him open and exposed, Paul could no more stop or pause than he could fly.

He lowered his lips to hers once more. As her tongue,

hungry and seeking, stole into his mouth, setting him on fire, he reached up and released her hair from its clip. Threading his fingers through the espresso waterfall of silky strands, he savored the spill of softness against his skin. He breathed in her vanilla scent as she roped her arms around his neck and murmured her appreciation. The sound popped a circuit in his brain, turning his thoughts into white noise that drowned out all things rational.

They tumbled onto her bed, hands skimming beneath the fabric of their clothes to the hot skin beneath. Groaning and panting, they deepened their kisses. Clothing fell away. Paul cupped Lia's breast and pulled her tight nipple into his mouth. With a wordless cry, she arched her back and shifted her hips in entreaty. He wanted to take his time, to put his mouth between her thighs and taste her arousal, but his hunger for her burned too hot. His hands shook as he slid on a condom and shifted her until she straddled him.

Her blissful expression transfixed him. Then she tossed her head back and lowered herself onto his erection. Engulfed by the heat of her, Paul forgot how to breathe. No woman he'd ever known had blindsided him like Lia. She aroused impulsive cravings that couldn't be denied and he'd long since lost the will to resist.

When her orgasm slammed into her, Paul felt the impact shake his soul. In the aftermath, he skimmed his palms over her flushed skin until her lashes lifted. Her eyes glowed with naked joy and absolute trust. At the sight, something rattled loose in his chest, stopping his heart.

"I…"

With a tender smile she set her fingertips against his lips. "Come for me. Please. I need you so much."

Keeping them locked together, Paul flipped Lia onto her back and began driving into her tight heat. With an ardent moan she drove her fingers into his hair and met his deep thrusts with a hunger and enthusiasm that turned his desire into something reckless and unstoppable. He locked his lips to hers and surged into her over and over, feasting on her pleas. She was on the verge of coming again when his climax built to a point of no return.

With her legs wrapped around his hips, her teeth grazing his neck, he held off until a series of tremors detonated through her body and she yielded a soft, keening cry of pleasure. Only then did he let himself be caught in the shattering brilliance of his orgasm.

Contentment settled over Paul as he buried his face in Lia's silky hair and waited for his breath to level out. Trailing his fingertips across her delicate shoulders and down her slender back, he stared at the tin ceiling, then turned his head and took in the cozy pillows they'd knocked to the floor with their passion. Reality intruded, banishing the hazy glow of satisfaction.

They'd agreed she would stay for two weeks. Seven days had already passed. The proof that she would soon depart was all around them. The truth in his heart was that Paul wasn't ready to let her go.

With the wedding Paul had invited her to only two days away, Lia took inventory of her closet and found nothing suitable for an evening wedding featuring a Charleston socialite and a multimillionaire. Dallas had described the private event as a "simple affair," but Lia guessed Charleston "simple" wasn't a barefoot bride in her momma's backyard with a barbecue picnic to follow. No, this wedding would be elegant and classy with a guest list that included the town's elite.

Lia wanted something that would let her blend in with the rest of the Southern women in attendance, but had no idea what that would be. Her best bet would be to reach out to Poppy and Dallas to see if they had recommendations. Once Lia had shot each woman a text, explaining her dilemma, their immediate and enthusiastic response left her second-guessing her decision. In just a few days she'd be bidding them goodbye. Growing closer to the twins was only going to make leaving harder. Not for her. She was all too accustomed to parting ways with those she'd grown fond of.

On the other hand, the Watts family was a tight-knit group who'd been devastated when Ava left. Of course, Grady's daughter had spent her whole life embraced by her family and naturally when she'd fled Charleston, her absence left a void. By the time the story came out that Lia wasn't actually Ava's daughter, they would only have known her for a couple weeks. The loss wouldn't be as profound.

While Lia was pondering her eventual break with the Watts family, she'd received a flurry of group texts. Dallas listed the names of several boutiques in downtown Charleston while Poppy chimed in with her opinion on each one. Lia read the messages with a growing sense of turmoil. At last she jumped in and asked if either one would be available later that afternoon to come shopping with her and give her some tips. An enthusiastic yes from both women left her overwhelmed with fondness and riddled with guilt.

At three o'clock Lia slid into the back seat of Dallas's large SUV while Poppy rode shotgun. The two women exchanged animated opinions as to what would be suitable for the wedding as Dallas drove.

At the first store the twins took her to, Lia could immediately see she was in the wrong place. The clothes had a sexy vibe that she might have explored if her goal was to stand out. When she said as much, the twins exchanged a puzzled look.

"But you've got the perfect body to rock all of this," Dallas said, indicating a short red-orange number with a plunging neckline.

"I don't see why you wouldn't want to show off what you've got," Poppy contributed.

"That's not the first impression I want to make," Lia said carefully. "I was thinking that I wanted to blend in."

"But that's so boring," Poppy cried.

"I think boring is just fine when it comes to a wedding," Lia countered.

"But we're already here. At least try on two things," Dallas said. "Even if you don't buy anything, it'll be fun to try some stuff on."

"Dallas and I will each pick something for you and you can see which you like better."

Poppy's enthusiasm quashed any further protest. What

would it hurt for her to indulge the twins? But even as Lia nodded her acceptance, she reflected on their growing camaraderie. Usually her nomadic lifestyle kept her from diving too deep into friendship, but the twins were engaging and endearing. From the first they'd made Lia feel like a part of their inner circle. The fact that she didn't belong, combined with her part in the deception, shadowed Lia's enjoyment of the outing. Still, the twins were a formidable distraction when they combined their persuasive powers and soon Lia surrendered to their enthusiasm.

They didn't allow her to do any browsing of her own and Lia could see that they'd played this game often with each other. Although they were identical twins, their personalities and styles couldn't have been more different. Where Dallas preferred pastel tones and floaty, ruffled dresses that moved as she walked, Poppy adopted a more casual style with bright fabrics that hugged her body and showed off all her assets.

Selections made, the twins herded Lia toward the dressing room. She entered the enclosed space and surveyed each outfit. The first was a strapless bedazzled dress in cobalt blue. While it was beautiful and would no doubt look great with her coloring, it screamed *look at me*. The second dress—a body-skimming red halter with high side split—was no better. If she walked into the party wearing this, everyone would see her and want to know who she was.

Still, Lia had agreed to try both on. She stepped out in the cobalt blue dress first.

"What do you think?" she asked, turning before the three-way mirror.

"I think all Paul's friends will be drooling over you," Dallas said.

That was the last thing Lia was looking for. She didn't want anyone singling her out.

"It's beautiful," she said. "But not exactly what I'm looking for. I feel a little too…" She tugged up the neckline, and then down on the hem. "I would feel a little too exposed in the dress."

"Try the red one on," Poppy said.

Lia returned to the dressing room and swapped dresses. Although the red halter was a little better, she still felt like she was trying too hard to send a message. She came out and had mixed reactions. While Poppy nodded vigorously, Dallas shook her head.

"The color is good on you and it really shows off the muscle tone in your arms, but that slit…"

"Agreed," Lia said. "Let's try somewhere else."

King Street was lined with boutiques and Lia soon learned that at some point, the twins had shopped them all. At the next store they went to the dresses were more in Dallas's style, with lace and ruffle details in pastel fabrics that made Lia look as if she was trying too hard to be someone she wasn't.

"I'm looking for something between these two stores," Lia said, worrying that she was never going to be able to find anything that suited her.

"I have a place in mind," Dallas said.

Lia changed back into her regular clothes and the three women departed for yet another boutique. As soon as they entered, Lia knew this was exactly where she needed to be. This time, instead of letting the twins choose, Lia intended to be part of the search for something she liked. There was a lot for her to pick from, but she settled on one dress in particular.

The gorgeous long-sleeved, ankle-length sheath fit her perfectly. A subtle sparkle ran through the blush-colored fabric that helped define her slender curves without drawing too much attention.

"This one," Lia said, exiting the dressing room to show off her pick.

"It's elegant and understated," Poppy said, but her expression reflected doubt. "Are you sure you don't want something with more pizzazz?"

"Elegant and refined is what I was going for," Lia said, gazing at her reflection in the mirror. "Unfortunately, I can't afford this dress. But you get the idea of what I'm going for."

"You shouldn't worry about the expense," Dallas said, highlighting the stark difference between how the twins lived and Lia's reality.

Despite the fact that both women held down jobs and paid their own expenses, they came from a wealthy family and this gave them a financial edge. Where Lia lived simply and sometimes had to scrape the bottom of her piggy bank when something unexpected happened, she knew all the twins had to do was dip into their extensive reserves.

"It's too much money to spend on something I can't imagine having the chance to wear again," Lia said, pretending not to see the look the twins exchanged.

Since the first day she'd met them, Lia had been dropping hints that she'd soon be leaving Charleston to get back on the road, preparing everyone for the moment when the testing mistake was revealed. Each time she mentioned leaving, one or more of the Wattses deflected her assertion, making it perfectly clear they didn't want her to go. Even though she recognized their affection for her was based on their belief that she was Ava's daughter, Lia had begun to dread the moment when she was no longer part of this family.

She'd always downplayed her need for an emotional support network. Her mother had instilled self-reliance in Lia from an early age. But looking at this way of life through the eyes of the Watts family, she'd started to see its limitations.

Bidding a determined farewell to the blush sheath, Lia settled on a markdown dress in black that skimmed her slim figure and highlighted her shoulders. Both Poppy and Dallas approved the sophisticated style, but best of all, the price was just inside her comfort zone. It wasn't the dress of her dreams but it would definitely do, and she couldn't wait to see Paul's expression when he saw her in it.

Ethan was heading home after another long day at Watts Shipping when he spied the open door to his father's large corner office and stepped inside. Instead of finding his father behind his large mahogany desk, Miles Watts stood near the windows, a drink in his hand, his gaze aimed toward the Cooper River, his mind far beyond the space he occupied.

"Wasn't Mom expecting you home hours ago?" Ethan asked, struck as always by how much Paul resembled his father with their matching tall frames, the family's distinct green eyes and wavy blond hair.

"No," Miles replied, shifting his gaze to his younger son. "She had book club tonight."

"I'm surprised you didn't take the opportunity to head to Chapins."

Chapins was a favorite of the Watts men. An upscale cigar lounge in the heart of downtown Charleston, it offered a large selection of rare and vintage brands.

"I had too much to do here," Miles said, gesturing toward his desk with the crystal tumbler. "Are you heading out?"

"I thought I'd swing by the gym before heading home." But instead of bidding his dad good-night, he advanced into the room. "Is everything okay? You seem distracted."

"Your mom brought one of her lemon pound cakes over to Grady today. You know how he loves her baking."

Ethan smiled. "We all do."

Miles nodded. "She ran into Taylor English while she was there."

While it wasn't unusual for Grady's attorney to visit him, something about the encounter had obviously prompted Ethan's mother to comment on it.

"And?" Ethan asked.

"And nothing." His father threw Ethan a dry look. "You know she wouldn't discuss her business with your grandfather."

"But Taylor must've said something that got you thinking, otherwise you wouldn't mention it."

"It wasn't what she told your mother, it was the questions she was asking about Lia, her background and if Paul had checked her out."

Ethan began to feel uneasy, but kept his tone neutral. "What did Mom tell her?"

"That she assumed Paul had vetted her." Miles glanced toward his son for confirmation before continuing. "But Taylor had all sorts of questions."

"Like what?"

"She pointed out the holes in Lia's adoption story. Would a court really give a baby to a woman who moved around so much? Isn't there a whole process that happens where she'd have to be evaluated for stability?"

"I'm sure that happened," Ethan interjected, wishing they'd concocted a more run-of-the-mill backstory instead of using Lia's actual past.

Ethan's father didn't look convinced. "Why would Taylor ask so many questions about Lia unless she suspected something was wrong?"

"You know what kind of lawyer Taylor is. She's thorough."

"But why would she need to be thorough? The testing service determined Lia is Ava's daughter. I don't understand why Taylor would question that." His father's eyes narrowed. "Unless she doesn't think the testing service is reliable. Your mother wondered if we should have our own DNA test run."

Although his father had just presented him with the perfect opportunity to explain about the mistake, Ethan hesitated to put an end to their scheme. They'd agreed to a couple weeks. Paul was acting as best man at Ryan and Zoe's wedding the next afternoon and had invited Lia to join him. Both deserved a heads-up before Ethan broke the news that Lia wasn't family.

"Is Taylor right to ask questions?" Miles demanded after Ethan took too long deciding how to answer. And then when Ethan continued to grapple with his conscience, his father cursed. "What is really going on with Lia?"

"Nothing."

Miles crossed his arms and glared. "Do not lie to me."

Ethan sucked in a deep breath and let it ease from his lungs. "Okay, here's the thing…" As he explained the situation, claiming complete responsibility for the scheme, his father stared at him in dismay.

"Damn it, Ethan," Miles raged as he kneaded the back of his neck. "This is the craziest stunt you've ever pulled. What were you thinking?"

"I did it for Grady," Ethan said, refusing to be treated like a reckless teenager. "And for Paul. Haven't you noticed that things between him and Grady have improved?"

Miles gave a reluctant nod. "And I'm glad, but you can't seriously be planning to pass Lia off as family forever."

"The plan was only supposed to last until Grady improved and he has. Everything will be over in a few days."

"Over how?"

Ethan's concern eased as he realized his father was willing to hear him out before deciding to blow the whistle. "We plan to announce that the testing service got it wrong and she's not Ava's daughter."

"That is going to devastate Dad."

"I know he'll be upset," Ethan said. "But I'm convinced that we would've lost him if he hadn't believed Lia was Ava's daughter. And he's stronger now. I think he'll be okay when he finds out the truth."

"You *hope* he'll be okay," Miles corrected. "Just be ready for the consequences, because if there are any setbacks in Grady's health, that's on Paul and you."

"Not Paul. Just me. By the time Paul found out what was going on we were too far in."

Miles leveled a keen stare on his younger son. "One last thing. You really need to tell your grandfather the whole truth."

Ethan shook his head. "I considered that, but decided that if Grady found out we tricked him on top of losing Ava's daughter, it would be a bigger blow."

"The problem with the whole DNA testing angle," Miles said, "is that Grady will believe Ava's daughter is still out there."

"I've been thinking about that." Ethan opened his briefcase and pulled out the test kit he'd ordered in the days after he'd concocted his scheme to pass Lia off as Grady's granddaughter. "Maybe you could help me find her for real."

Eight

The morning of his best friend's wedding, Paul spent a few hours at the office, but found he couldn't concentrate. That had been happening all too often in the days since that long afternoon in Lia's camper. Despite the unusual surroundings, or maybe because of them, Paul knew the time with Lia was indelibly etched in his memories. They'd made love for hours, forgoing new truck shopping and skipping dinner. Only after their exertions made their hunger for food more urgent than their appetite for each other did they get dressed and grab a couple burgers at a fast-food restaurant.

He hadn't been exaggerating: giving in to their attraction was going to complicate things. She wasn't like any woman he'd ever known and he hadn't crossed the line with her lightly. This left him with a dilemma.

Sneaking around with her compounded his discomfort about the lies they were perpetrating. But the thought of giving her up left him in an ill-tempered funk.

Following the compulsion to see her, Paul left his office and drove to his grandfather's estate. The sound of feminine laughter reached his ears as he exited his SUV, luring him toward the pool. Expecting to find his cousins clad in their customary bikinis, lazily floating on rafts in the turquoise water, he was besieged by wonder and a trace of amusement at what greeted him instead.

His cousins and Lia balanced on paddleboards in the middle of the pool, engaged in yoga moves. While both Dallas and Poppy wore bathing suits, Lia was dressed in her daily uniform of black yoga pants and a graphic T-shirt that flattered her lean curves and drew attention to her high, firm breasts. Given that both his cousins had wet hair and were wobbling dangerously on the ever-shifting boards while trying to hold a standing yoga pose, Paul assumed it must be much harder than Lia was making it look.

She moved fluidly on the board, shifting from one pose to another with barely a ripple in the pool. Her confidence fascinated him. At every turn she surprised him with a whole range of unexpected talents from cake decorating to accompanying Grady's drumming on the harmonica to assorted art projects geared toward children that now adorned Grady's bedroom.

With each day that passed, she endeared herself to his entire family more and more, and even Paul's high level of skepticism had failed him. Lia was a whirling dervish of energy and optimism and it was hard to remain detached, especially when every time they occupied the same room, she became the focal point of his awareness. His determined distrust had given way beneath the pressure of the undeniable energy between them. The maddening chemistry was more than sexual. The hunger to be near her was a fire that burned throughout his entire body.

He found her stories of life on the road fascinating. Her kindness toward his grandfather wasn't an act. Every minute Paul spent in her company boosted his optimism and lightened his mood. The tiniest brush of his hand against hers sent a shower of sparks through him. Dozens of times he'd caught himself on the verge of touching her in front of his family. Whenever they occupied the same room, he had to struggle to keep his gaze from lingering on her.

Spying Grady in the shade of the pool house, Paul approached and sat down beside his grandfather's wheelchair. Grady reached out and gave Paul's arm an affectionate squeeze. With the return of his grandfather's love and approval, Paul had no more need to arm himself against the grief that had caused him to guard against personal relationships. Another positive change in his life he could attribute to Lia. Was there no end to her uplifting influence? Did he really want there to be?

Once again Paul was struck by concern for what the future might hold after Lia's departure. While Grady grew more robust with each passing day, finding out that Lia wasn't his granddaughter was certain to hit him hard. Would his depression return?

"What are they doing?" he asked, crossing his ankle

over his knee as the afternoon's humid air made its way beneath the collar of his navy polo.

"Yoga," Grady sang, bright amusement in the gaze he flicked toward his grandson.

"Why are they doing it on paddleboards in the middle of the pool?"

"Harder."

Seeing Grady's fond smile, Paul felt a familiar stab of guilt that they were perpetrating a fraud on the old man. His grandfather loved Lia because he believed she was his long-lost granddaughter. That she wasn't ate at Paul more every day.

"I can see that. The twins look like they're struggling."

Even as he spoke, Poppy lost her balance, but before she tumbled into the pool, she dropped to her knees and clutched the edges of the board. She laughed in relief while Dallas and Lia called out their encouragement.

Paul guessed this wasn't Lia's first time doing this because she was rock-solid on the board. "It's good to see you outside," Paul said, tearing his gaze away from her. "How are you feeling today?"

"I'm feeling strong." Grady spoke the words with triumph.

"You're getting better every day," Paul murmured. "That's wonderful."

The two men sat in companionable silence and watched the three women for another half hour, until Lia brought the session to a halt.

"Nice work, ladies," she called, towing the paddleboards toward the storage room at the back of the pool house while his cousins toweled off.

Paul went to help her, eager for a couple seconds alone, somewhere out of the way so he didn't have to guard his expression. He took in the light sheen of moisture coating her skin, tempting him to ride his palms over her sun-warmed arms and around her waist. If he dipped his head and slid his tongue along her neck, he knew she would taste salty. His mouth watered at the memory of her silky flesh beneath his lips.

"You've done that before," Paul said, letting her precede him into the large room crammed with pool toys.

"My mother teaches yoga. I've been doing it since I could stand," Lia said. "You should try it. Besides increasing flexibility and muscle tone, it can reduce stress."

He paused in the act of stacking the boards against the back wall. "Do I seem stressed to you?"

"I was thinking maybe you'd like to improve your flexibility," she teased, shooting him a wry grin.

Paul nodded, letting her score the point without retaliating. She wouldn't be the first person who'd described him as intractable. It's what enabled him to keep pursuing criminals when the trail went cold. At the same time, he recognized being obstinate had created problems in his relationship with his family.

"Grady seems to be doing better every day," he remarked, reaching for her hand. As their fingers meshed, his entire body sighed with delight at the contact. "It's hard to believe that less than two weeks ago we were all worried he wasn't going to last until the end of the month."

"You know he's really proud of you."

His gut twisted at her words. "I don't know that."

"Well, he is," she said, her thumb stroking across his knuckles.

"Even though I didn't join the family business?"

"It makes him happy that you're passionate about what you do." Lia's warm smile eased the tightness in Paul's chest. "And that you help people by making the world safer."

"Thank you," Paul said, tugging her closer.

Entreaty flickered in her eyes, quickly masked by her long dark lashes. His blood heated as he detected an unsteadiness in her breathing. Damn, he badly wanted to kiss her. The need to claim her soft mouth overwhelmed him. Not even the worry that they might be caught could temper the wild emotions she aroused.

Acting before he could convince himself that it was madness, Paul backed Lia toward the wall. A surprised whoosh of air escaped her as her spine connected with the hard surface. He skimmed his fingers down her arms, pinned her wrists to the wall on either side of her hips.

Curses momentarily drowned out his thoughts. "We should get back to the pool before someone comes looking for us."

Releasing his grip on her, Paul flattened his palms against the wall and started to push away, but her reflexes proved faster than his. Before he could escape, she'd locked her hands around his back and tugged him even closer.

"Kiss me first." Her lips curved in a sassy grin that was equal parts sexy and sweet. "Unless you don't want to."

He almost laughed at her words. Not only did he *want* to kiss her, he *needed* to kiss her. Needed it like the air he breathed and the food he ate. She was the most irritating, frustrating female he'd ever known. Thoughts of her distracted him all the time. It took effort to concentrate on his job and for that he couldn't forgive her. Worse, he was ravenous for her in a way that couldn't be denied and with each day his willpower weakened.

Her eagerness was a temptation he couldn't resist and Paul found himself swept into the kiss. Into her warmth and sweetness and enthusiasm. He took what she gave. Unable to stop. Unwilling to stop.

Paul wasn't sure what brought him back from the brink, but soon he lifted his lips from hers and trailed kisses across her cheek.

"I can't stop thinking about being with you again," he murmured, surprising himself with the admission. "But you have that birthday party at the hospital this afternoon, don't you?"

Her chest rose and fell as she stared at him, her beautiful hazel eyes wide and utterly trusting. "You remembered."

Paul stepped back and raked his fingers through his hair. "Do you mind if I tag along?"

"You're always welcome to be my knight-errant."

Even as warmth pooled in his gut, the urge to warn

her to be careful of him rose. The things he wanted to do to her weren't romantic or chivalrous. Her love of dressing up as a princess drove home the intrinsic sentimental nature of her true soul.

In fairy tales, princesses got rescued from towers, endless sleep and villains who intended them harm. Paul was no Prince Charming. In fact, he'd acted more like a beast with Lia. And even if his initial disdain had given way to grudging admiration, he didn't deserve her trust.

"That's fine as long as I don't have to wear tights," he grumbled and neither her surprised laughter nor her affectionate hug improved his mood.

On a normal visit to the children's ward at the hospital, Lia would've lost herself in the part of Elsa, the Snow Queen. Bringing joy to children, especially ones who needed to escape reality for a little while, gave her own spirits an enormous boost. But Paul's solemn gaze on her the entire time made her all too aware of the heat and confusion between them.

Every stolen moment with him pushed her further into uncharted territory. She'd never known the sort of urgent craving he aroused in her. In the past, she'd always viewed sex as a pleasurable way to connect with someone she cared about. What she experienced with Paul turned every other encounter into a foggy memory. The crystal-pure clarity of his fingers gliding over her skin. The keen pleasure of his weight pressing her into the mattress. His deep kisses and soul-stirring moans as he slid into her. All of it was etched into her soul never to be forgotten.

Yet all too soon she'd be leaving Charleston, never to see him again. Lia wasn't sure what to do about her growing resistance to the idea of resuming her travels. Never before had she faced a compulsion to stay put. But her growing attachment to Paul was a big part of that. Normally Lia would blindly follow her heart, but this time she recognized that trusting her instincts was impossible. She'd mired herself in a scheme that had only one outcome. Once the genetic test was revealed to be flawed, no member of the Watts family would want her to stick around.

Not even Paul. Despite her longing for a relationship to developing with him, she feared that if she remained in Charleston, eventually her past would come between them. He'd dedicated his career to hunting criminals. She could imagine his fury when he discovered her grandfather was in prison. And learning what had put him there would confirm Paul's initial opinion of her as an opportunist.

Part of her recognized he was probably still digging into her background. She'd be wise to tell him the truth and face his displeasure before her growing feelings for him made heartbreak inevitable, but as they walked back to the estate, Lia lost her nerve. She was gambling that he wouldn't turn up anything with less than a week until she left Charleston. Better that she stay silent so that his memories of her remained unsullied.

They parted company at the driveway and Lia headed for the house. Upon entering her bedroom, she spied something that hadn't been there when she'd left. A garment bag, twin to the one from the boutique hanging on the armoire door, lay across her bed, along with an envelope. Puzzled, Lia set aside her long ice-blue gloves, opened the envelope and read the note.

We know you loved this dress and wanted you to have it.—Dallas & Poppy.

Overwhelmed by the twins' generosity, Lia slowly unfastened the bag's zipper to reveal the stunning blush gown she'd fallen in love with. Guilt clawed at her. She shouldn't accept the gift. The twins had purchased the expensive dress believing she was their real cousin. Yet to refuse would force awkward explanations.

Lia wanted to scream in frustration. Why did everyone have to be so kind to her? The deception would've been so much simpler if she'd been greeted with the same sort of suspicion that Paul had demonstrated.

After shooting the twins an effusive thank-you text, Lia jumped in the shower. As she applied her makeup and experimented with several hairstyles, she tried to ignore her anxiety over what she might encounter at the upcoming event. Pretending to be Ava's daughter had grown easier these last few days. Not that her subterfuge rode any easier on her conscience, but once she'd answered the tricky questions surrounding her childhood to everyone's satisfaction, she'd been able to lower her guard somewhat.

But attending this wedding with Paul meant she would be under scrutiny once more. Although he'd promised his circle of friends wouldn't ask too many questions about her, Lia suspected that they'd be wildly speculative about any woman he'd bring. Once again, the opportunity to spend more time in his company was a temptation she couldn't resist. Hopefully it wouldn't backfire on them.

The dress fit as perfectly as when she'd tried it on in the shop, reviving Lia's confidence. Tonight she would demonstrate to Paul that she could at least appear as if she fit into his social circle, even if she'd be completely out of her element. As long as she smiled a lot, said little and stuck like glue to Paul's side, she should be fine.

Lia arrived in the formal living room five minutes before she was scheduled to meet Paul only to discover that he'd beaten her there. She had a fraction of a second to appreciate the way his charcoal-gray suit fit his imposing figure and to indulge in a little delighted swoon before he glanced up from his phone and swept a heated gaze over her.

The possessive approval Lia saw there stripped her of her ability to speak or move. As often as she'd donned a costume and played the role of a princess, she'd never truly felt like one before. But now, as she basked in Paul's admiration, she understood what it meant to be treasured.

"You look gorgeous," Paul said, walking over to her. Clearly cautious over the possibility that anyone could stumble on them, he limited his contact to a brief squeeze of her fingers, but even that fleeting touch sent Lia's pulse into overdrive. "I'll have to stay close tonight or my friends will try to lure you away."

"Oh." His low murmur set the butterflies fluttering in her stomach. "No." She shook her head as the full import of his words struck her.

"No?" He looked taken aback.

She shook her head and rushed to explain. "I didn't think I'd stand out in this dress."

Paul's posture relaxed once more. A sensual smile curved his chiseled lips. "You stand out no matter what you wear."

With her skin flushing at his compliment, Lia slid a little deeper into infatuation. Even so, she recognized that the easing of Paul's earlier distrust gave his approval greater significance. Still, there was no fighting the inevitable. She was falling hard for his man.

He took her by the elbow and propelled her toward the door, his confidence muffling her concern. "Relax, you'll be fine."

"That's easy for you to say," she muttered grimly. "This is your world." And she didn't belong.

Twenty minutes later, Lia's mood had lightened. During the short drive to one of the most impressive mansions in Charleston's historic district Paul had shared Ryan and Zoe's inspirational path to love.

Long before the pair met, Zoe had been in the middle of a scandalous divorce. To appear the wounded party and avoid having to pay her alimony, her husband had publicly accused Zoe of infidelity. Eventually the truth of her innocence came out, but by then her reputation was ruined and her finances were in tatters.

Devastated and bitter, Zoe had joined a revenge bargain with two strangers, women who'd also been wronged by powerful men. To deflect suspicion, each woman was tasked with taking down a man she had no connection to. In Zoe's case, her target had been Ryan and she was supposed to hurt him by damaging his sister's political career.

Zoe hadn't counted on the romance that bloomed with Ryan or the difficulty in extricating herself from the vengeance pact. In the end, because Zoe hadn't been directly responsible for the resulting scandal that harmed Ryan's family, he'd chosen to put aside his anger, unable to imagine a future without her in it.

Paul obviously approved of the union despite its rocky beginning, leading Lia to hope he could set aside his stubborn and judgmental nature when faced with true happiness.

As soon as they went inside, the soothing strains of a string quartet enveloped them. Lush floral arrangements in warm shades of peach and pink decorated every room on the main floor. Lia inhaled the richly scented air as they strolled through the various rooms on their way to the rear garden where the ceremony would be taking place.

Paul introduced her to several people before his best man duties called him away. He left her with Zoe's former brother-in-law the race car driver Harrison Crosby and his fiancée, London McCaffrey. Lia appreciated the couple's easy acceptance of her company as they sipped preceremony champagne before making their way to the area in the garden where the chairs had been set up for the wedding.

The ceremony was short but beautiful. The bride wore a romantic confection of tulle embellished with lace flowers. Her groom stood beside Paul in a charcoal suit and pink bow tie, looking positively gobsmacked as she walked up the aisle toward him. They were emotional as they exchanged vows, bringing both smiles and tears to the thirty or so guests who'd come to celebrate with them.

Lia was still dabbing tears from her eyes when Paul came to find her after the ceremony.

"Are you okay?" he asked, arching an eyebrow at her.

"It was a beautiful wedding," she whispered. "They're so obviously in love."

"They came through a lot to get here," he murmured, his gaze following the bride and groom as they greeted friends and accepted congratulations. "I think it's made them stronger as a couple."

Struck by both his sentiment and the show of obvious affection for his friends, Lia exclaimed, "Paul Watts, you are a romantic!"

He frowned at her accusation. "I wouldn't say that."

"Don't deny it." A happy glow enveloped her. "Here I expected you to have a suspicious view of the whole love-and-marriage thing and you go all mushy on me."

"I'm not mushy."

She ignored his growled denial. "I never imagined you'd be a fan of love and such."

"Calling me a fan is a little over-the-top," he protested, taking her by the elbow and turning her toward the house where the reception dinner and after-party were taking place. "And why is it so surprising that I believe in love?"

"Love requires a leap of faith," she explained, having mulled this topic often in the last few days. "You're so logical."

He looked thoughtful as he considered her point. "It's also about trust," he said, indicating he'd also given the matter some consideration. "Trust of yourself and of the other person."

"But you're not exactly the trusting sort," she reminded him.

"That's not completely accurate when it comes to family and friends."

His single-minded, fierce protectiveness of those closest to him was sexy as hell. She was used to being alone and never considered what it might be like with someone to count on. Lately, however, Lia had pondered the immense sense of security those closest to Paul must feel. She'd never doubted that he was someone who could be counted on to aid and protect, but until now hadn't considered what being the beneficiary of such attention might be like.

That afternoon in her camper, encircled by his strong arms, she'd experienced a sense of well-being unlike anything she'd ever known. At the time she'd put the sensation down to their lovemaking and her joy at being inside the familiar refuge of her camper.

But maybe it had been just as much about gaining Paul's trust. Watching him with his family had offered her insight into his protective nature. He wanted nothing but the best for those he loved. When he'd begun to open up to her in small ways, she'd been thrilled to be gifted with this show of faith.

"So what you're saying," she clarified, "is that once given, your trust is complete?" The power of that took her breath away. "What if someone does something that goes against your principles?"

She was thinking about how Ethan had plotted to introduce her as Grady's granddaughter and the hit Paul was taking to his integrity in going along with the scheme. Yet the animosity between the brothers originated with Ethan. Paul obviously loved his brother and hated their estrangement.

"As much as I wish everything was black-and-white, it's never that simple." Paul stopped beside their assigned places at the dinner table and drew out her chair. "Now, can we drop all this serious talk and have some fun?"

With a nod, Lia abandoned the topic and focused her attention on enjoying the delicious reception dinner Dallas had prepared and marveling at the change in Paul as he socialized with his close friends, trading good-natured quips and contributing his share of funny stories that stretched back to their grade school days.

The depth and breadth of connection these people shared highlighted Lia's isolation. An ache grew in her chest that she recognized as longing. She wanted to belong. To feel the snug embrace of camaraderie. To be in on the private jokes and accepted into the club.

But this was an exclusive group of people, and not just because they'd been friends since childhood. Each one possessed an easy confidence born of privilege. In contrast was Lia as she sat beside Paul, listening attentively while speaking little, a huge fraud in the dress she couldn't afford.

As the waitstaff set plates of wedding cake before

all the guests, Lia excused herself and headed to the bathroom. On the way back to the dining room, Dallas appeared in her path. As Lia gushed over the delicious dinner, she immediately sensed that Paul's cousin wasn't paying the least amount of attention to her compliments.

"Is something wrong?" Lia asked, uneasiness sliding across her nerve endings at the older twin's somber expression.

"You and Paul…" Dallas began, her voice scarcely rising above a whisper. "I saw what happened between you when you were putting the paddleboards away."

Cheeks flaming, Lia thought back to those stolen moments. It was her fault that they'd been caught. She'd begged him to kiss her.

"You two were…" Dallas looked horrified. "Kissing."

Lia threw up her hands as if to ward off the undeclared accusation. "It's not what you think—"

"You're first cousins."

"We're not." Stricken by Dallas's accusation, Lia blurted out the denial without considering the wisdom of spilling the truth before she'd spoken to Paul and Ethan about it.

Dallas frowned. "I don't understand."

Lia clutched her evening bag to her chest, struggling with the dilemma she found herself in. "There's a problem with my DNA test results," she declared in a breathless rush, sick of all the lies. "Ethan and Paul know, but you can't tell anyone else."

"What sort of a problem?"

"I'm not your long-lost cousin." Lia crossed her fingers and hoped that Ethan and Paul wouldn't be angry with her for jumping the gun. "We just found out that there was a huge mix-up."

Dallas looked appalled. "Why haven't you told anyone?"

"Because Grady has rallied since he thought I was his granddaughter and we've been waiting for him to be fully on the path to recovery before saying anything."

"He's going to be so upset," Dallas said. "He's been obsessed with finding Ava's daughter."

Lia hung her head. "We know."

"I can't believe Paul would let this go on."

"He's not happy about it, believe me." Lia grabbed Dallas's hand. "Please don't tell anyone. We've agreed that I'm only going to stay another few days."

"And then what?"

"Then we come clean about the mistake and I get back on the road."

Dallas stared at her in silence while emotions flitted across her face. "I don't understand any of this," she complained at last. "Why do you have to leave?"

"I was never going to stay," Lia reminded her, repeating what she'd been saying all along. "I like traveling the country too much to stay put anywhere."

"But Grady loves you. We all do."

"He loves his granddaughter," Lia said, her heart aching at the thought of moving on. Never before had she grieved for her lack of family ties. "I'm not her."

"What about Paul?"

"What about him?"

"You're obviously the woman from his reading. The one he's supposed to fall in love with."

"No." Lia ignored her pounding heart. "He's not in love with me. Attracted maybe, but we're too different to ever work."

"I think you might be exactly what he needs."

"Are you listening to yourself?" The laugh Lia huffed out fell flat. "A moment ago you were worried he and I were doing something creepy and wrong."

"That's when I thought you were our cousin," Dallas said. "Now that I know you're not, I heartily approve of you two."

"There is no *us two*," Lia corrected, her desperation growing by the second. "Please don't speak about this to anyone. Not even Poppy."

"But we tell each other everything."

"I know, but for now the fewer people who know, the better. And everything will come out in a matter of days." Seeing Dallas was still waffling, Lia gripped her hand. "Please."

"Fine," Dallas groused. "But you really should think about staying. For Paul's sake. And yours."

As Lia returned to Paul, she debated whether to tell him about her conversation with Dallas. She hated to let secrets and subterfuge get between them, but worried that he would keep his distance if he discovered that his cousin had caught them. With her time in Charleston growing short, she selfishly wanted to soak up his company and if he thought his cousin knew about their deception, that would preoccupy him to the exclusion of all else. She would just have to ensure that they were more careful around his family.

"Is everything okay?" Paul asked, his green eyes roaming her expression.

"Fine." Lia slid into her seat and hid her disquiet beneath a weary smile. "Just a little tired."

"Do you want me to take you home?"

Home. The word sent a spike of electricity through her. She knew he meant his grandfather's estate, but her home was a nineteen-foot camper parked north of the city. A few days from now she'd be hitting the road once more.

"Or maybe back to your house," she said, pushing aside all thoughts of leaving and the disquiet it aroused. "I'd love to spend some time alone with you."

"It's like you read my mind," he murmured. "Let's go."

Nine

The morning after Ryan and Zoe's wedding, Paul was up at dawn, retracing the walk along the beach he and Lia had taken the previous night before he'd dropped her off at the Watts estate. Her mood after leaving the wedding had been reflective, but when he'd asked her what was on her mind, she'd stopped his questions with a passionate kiss.

They'd made love for hours while the moon rose and spilled its pale light across his bedroom floor. He marveled how being in her company kept him grounded in the moment, his thoughts drifting over her soft skin, his focus locked on her fervent cries and the way her body shuddered in climax beneath him.

He'd been loath to take her back to his grandfather's house. Although they'd been together for hours, the time passed too quickly. He wanted to keep her in his bed. To wake up to her sweet face and bury his nose in her fragrant hair. Alone atop the tangled sheets that smelled of her perfume and their lovemaking, he'd spent the rest of a sleepless night staring at the ceiling and probing the dissatisfaction that dominated his mood.

What became crystal clear was that he didn't want Lia to leave. Not that night. Not in a few days. Maybe never.

Now as he looked out at the water this morning, he flashed back to the tarot card reading. The reversed Hermit card, indicating his time of being alone was over. The Lovers in his near future. The final outcome card promising happiness and joy. But there had also been the possible outcome card of the bound woman who Lia said represented confusion and isolation. He had a choice to make. Either maintain his current priorities by giving all his time and energy to his business or take a more balanced approach and open himself to the potential of love.

Appalled at himself for remembering all that New Age nonsense much less giving it the slightest bit of credibility, Paul returned home, showered and then sat down in his home office to lose himself in work. Although he had staff to follow through with the day-to-day business of protecting their clients' data, Paul liked to keep his skill level up to date. As fast as they plugged one hole, the criminals found another to get through.

The morning passed in a blur. He'd left his phone in the kitchen to avoid the temptation to call Lia. Around noon his stomach began to growl so he went into the kitchen to make some lunch.

Ethan had messaged him, asking how the wedding had gone and inviting him for an afternoon of fishing. The offer delighted Paul. It had been a long time since he'd hung out with his brother and he missed the fun times they'd had.

After a quick text exchange to accept, Paul headed west to James Island. Ethan lived in a sprawling four-year-old custom-built house that backed up onto Ellis Creek and offered direct access to Ashley River and Charleston Harbor. With its white siding and navy shutters, reclaimed heart pine floors, white woodwork throughout including kitchen cabinets and built-ins, the home had a more traditional style than Paul expected from Ethan.

A mix of antiques and new furniture filled the rooms, offering a comfortable but conservative feel. Only one room had a purely masculine vibe and that was the entertainment room on the lower level. The room's dark brown walls and red ceiling were the back-drop for a large projection screen, sports-related art and pool table with red felt.

It was in this room Paul found his brother waiting. Because Ethan liked to entertain, the room's location on the creek side of the garage with direct access from the driveway meant that Ethan's friends could come and go from the party spot without traipsing through his entire house.

"So I've been thinking," Paul began, accepting the beer his brother handed him from the beverage cooler built into the wet bar.

"When are you not thinking?" Ethan countered. He

flopped onto the leather sectional and took a long pull from his bottle.

Ignoring his brother's jab, Paul rolled the bottle between his hands and paced. "Grady is progressing, but he's far from back to full health."

Ethan's eyebrow rose. "And?"

"We're due to tell everyone there's been the mix-up with Lia's genetic test in a few days and I'm just worried it's too soon and that he'll regress." For the hundredth time Paul wished Lia hadn't had such a profound effect on Grady's health. If she'd never come to stay at the estate, Paul could continue to pretend that he was perfectly content, never knowing how right he felt in her company, never knowing the all-consuming hunger or the raw joy of making love to her. She'd twisted his perceptions and made him question beliefs that ruled his life. Yet he couldn't get over the sense that she was the missing piece that made him whole.

"So you want her to stay longer?" Ethan asked, his eyes narrowing.

"Grady is happy." Paul spoke with deliberate care. "Because he thinks his granddaughter is back."

"I thought you were worried that he'd get too attached."

Paul let out a frustrated sigh, hating that he found himself trapped between a rock and a hard place. "That ship sailed the moment we didn't tell Grady the truth." He paused and drank his beer, picturing his grandfather by the pool the day before, the amused fondness in his gaze as he watched what he thought to be his three granddaughters.

"I don't know," Ethan muttered, sounding more like

Paul than Paul at the moment. "The longer we let this go the more we risk the truth coming out. Grady might never forgive us if he thinks we tricked him."

Paul couldn't believe the way the tables had turned. Usually he was the one sounding the alarm. "He'll never know."

"He'll never know?" Ethan echoed, looking doubtful. "What's gotten into you?"

"What do you mean?"

"You were dead set against her pretending to be Ava's daughter at all. Next you'll be suggesting she should stay permanently."

Ethan's remark was a hit Paul didn't see coming.

"Now that's a really bad idea." Paul trusted that he could keep his attraction hidden for another week or two, but pretending she was his first cousin wasn't a long-term solution. In fact, it was more like endless hell. "We can't keep lying to the whole family about her being Ava's daughter."

"About that…" Ethan stared out the windows that overlooked his expansive back lawn. "We're no longer lying to the *whole* family."

Ethan's statement was a streaking comet along Paul's nerve endings. "What does that mean?"

"It means that Mom ran into Taylor English the other day and she had a lot of questions about how Lia's mom came to adopt her."

"Do you think Taylor suspects that Lia's not Ava's daughter?"

"Maybe. I don't know. Mom shared her concerns

with Dad and he was worried. So…" A muscle flexed in Ethan's jaw. "I told Dad the truth."

"Damn it, Ethan."

"He suggested running another DNA test," his brother retorted in a reasonable tone that Paul found irritating. "And I was able to explain what we're doing and why. It took some convincing, but I reminded Dad that Grady was on the verge of slipping away from us before he started believing his granddaughter had returned."

Paul sputtered through a string of curses, until the revelation of what Ethan had not said sank in. "He knows we lied about Lia, but he hasn't told anyone?"

"He hasn't told Grady," Ethan said, his precise wording catching Paul's attention. "But I'm guessing he told Mom."

"And his sister?"

"I don't think so," Ethan said. "Can you imagine Aunt Lenora keeping that secret to herself? She might be able to avoid letting it slip with Uncle Wiley, but she talks to the twins about everything."

"Okay." Paul rubbed his temple where a dull ache had developed. "So, you explained the plan to Dad and he was willing to keep Lia's true identity a secret?"

"For a few days." Ethan finished his beer and set it aside. "So you can see why it's probably not a good idea to ask Lia to stay longer."

"Just one more week can't hurt," Paul said, convinced he couldn't make a decision about Lia in a few days. "I'll talk to Dad."

Ethan looked doubtful. "You should also check with Lia. She's pretty keen to get back on the road."

"Speaking of that," Paul said. "I think we should revisit how much we're paying her."

Ethan studied him for a long moment before nodding. "Okay. But I thought you believed she was only in it for the money."

Paul made a dismissive gesture. "That was before I got to know her better."

"How much better?" Ethan demanded, his eyes narrowing.

"Well enough," Paul retorted, unwilling to expound on the time he'd spent in Lia's company. He pivoted the conversation back to something he was comfortable discussing. "She can't leave town without a truck to pull her camper. I've been thinking that our grandfather's health is worth a whole lot more than a brand-new truck, don't you?"

"Okay. Let's get her a truck with all the bells and whistles." Ethan got off the couch and headed for the beverage cooler. "Just don't be surprised when she decides against sticking around longer after she has the means to leave."

Ethan's warning plunged deep into the heart of what had been bothering Paul for days. He didn't want Lia to disappear out of his life. The free-spirited nomad had entangled him in her quirky web of metaphysical nonsense and selfless generosity. Where he kept to himself and focused on business, she told fortunes, spread joy and showered positive energy on everyone she met.

He had yet to decide if being complete opposites

would work for or against their romantic future. Since meeting her, Paul had begun noticing the concerns of those around him. He'd spent more time with his family in the last week than he had in the last few months. While he'd done so initially in order to keep an eye on Lia, as his suspicions about her faded, he'd realized how much he enjoyed interacting with his family.

"Do you think the lack of a vehicle is the only thing keeping her in Charleston?" Paul asked.

"That's always been the impression she's given me." Ethan paused and regarded Paul with raised eyebrows. "Has she indicated that she's ready to give up the road?"

"No." And that was the problem. "But you've known her longer. I thought perhaps she'd mentioned what it would take for her to settle down."

Ethan hit him with an odd look. "Why are you so interested?"

"It's just…"

Asking Ethan for romantic advice was harder than he expected. Paul didn't have a lot of practice putting his feelings into words. Nor was he good at sharing what was bothering him. That he wanted to try was another example of Lia's influence.

"Are you asking because you're attracted to her?" Ethan asked.

Feeling cornered, Paul kept his expression neutral. "She's pretending to be our first cousin." Yet he couldn't deny that it was getting harder and harder to avoid letting his feelings for her show.

"She's not our first cousin, though," Ethan countered. "And once the truth comes out the situation will get even more complicated. She's not going to want to stick around."

"No one will blame her for the testing service getting it wrong. Let's just see if she'll delay leaving for another week." Seeing his brother's worried expression, Paul added, "For Grady's sake."

"I'll talk to her," Ethan said. "But you need to be clear about what you want. Lia isn't someone you can toy with until an exciting project comes along that takes all your focus and energy."

"What are you saying?" Paul demanded, bristling at his brother's criticism.

"That if you're leading her on, you can do a lot of damage in a very short period of time."

Even though Ethan had invited his brother to go fishing, by the time their conversation concluded neither one was in the mood to take the boat out. Instead, after Paul left, Ethan wandered into his home office and contemplated the second genetic testing kit he'd ordered, but hadn't yet used.

As much as he wanted to satisfy the ever-intensifying craving to connect with his biological family, he recognized the revelations could come at a cost. Not only did he risk upsetting the people who loved him, but also he could be opening himself up to disappointment and heartbreak. Ethan couldn't explain his pessimism over the outcome, but recognized that not taking the test left him no better or worse off than he was at the moment.

And after watching Paul struggle with his fears and

desires concerning Lia, Ethan was even more wary of throwing himself into an emotional maelstrom.

When he'd introduced Lia to his family as Ava's daughter, the last thing Ethan had imagined was that Paul would complicate the situation by developing feelings for her. Paul was too logic-driven to appreciate Lia's spiritual nature and too skeptical to ever trust her motives for helping them. Then again, physical attraction was a powerful thing and could lead to an emotional connection. Even in someone as jaded and pragmatic as Paul.

While Ethan enjoyed seeing his guarded older brother thrown off-balance, concern for Lia tempered Ethan's satisfaction. Although she claimed that traveling around so much kept her from getting too attached to those she met, Ethan sensed that this time was different. If Lia fell for Paul the way he appeared to be falling for her, she'd throw her heart and soul at him and if Paul didn't wise up, she might end up hurt.

Turning away from the complicated and messy ramifications of his actions, Ethan focused on the trio of good things that had resulted. Grady's improved health. The healing rift between Paul and his grandfather. And one that Ethan hadn't expected, but found himself grateful for—the renewed connection with his brother.

Ethan hadn't realized the cost of pushing Paul away until the scheme with Lia had brought them together again. Setting his fingertips on the genetic testing kit, Ethan shoved it away. Maybe it was time to appreciate the family who loved him and not chase something that might not be out there.

* * *

The Sunday morning after Ryan and Zoe's wedding dawned as clear and golden as so many others Lia had experienced in her sumptuous bedroom. Despite her late return to the estate, she was awake with the sun. On a typical morning, she would bound out of bed and begin her day with yoga on the terrace overlooking the lush garden. But today didn't feel typical. Her mind raced, but her body felt sluggish. She curled herself around a pillow and clung to the glow from the previous night with Paul.

Three short days from now the news would break that she wasn't Grady's granddaughter, freeing her from the lies and obligations keeping her in Charleston. In the beginning, with Paul treating her like a criminal, Lia had dreaded the deception and longed for the moment when she could get back on the road. The sheer size and elegance of the Watts estate, not to mention the rules and traditions that operated within its walls, had been overwhelming. She wasn't used to being around people so much and missed the long hours of solitude to meditate or read or daydream.

But one thing that all her traveling to new towns had instilled in Lia was adaptability. Her acquaintances and jobs were constantly changing. So she'd learned how to function within the tight-knit Watts clan with their frequent visits to check on Grady, outgoing natures, busybody ways. And to her surprise, she'd started to enjoy the fun-loving twins, the kind mothering of Lenora and Constance and even Paul's unsettling presence.

Confronted with the reality that she would soon be

leaving it all behind, sadness sat like a large stone in her stomach, weighing her down. Yet she couldn't deny there was relief, as well. Living with the lie that she was Grady's granddaughter made her anxious and her attraction to Paul complicated everything.

With her emotions seesawing with each breath she took, Lia struggled to maintain her usual equanimity as she ate with Grady on the back terrace. She knew his family credited her with his daily improvement, but Lia put the credit squarely on his shoulders. His determination was only matched by his enthusiasm to try anything she'd suggested. The singing that had worked in the beginning hadn't been the only method to help him communicate. She'd created a notebook of common words and phrases that he could point to, which sped up conversations and eased frustration all around.

Grady had improved to the point that he intended to join the family for dinner that night. Leaving him to rest, Lia took a taxi to a nearby discount auto sales lot where she'd identified a truck that she hoped might be a good fit. The price was higher than she'd anticipated paying, but she was running out of time to find something that could pull Misty. Unfortunately, when she got to the lot, she discovered that the vehicle had already been sold, and nothing else they had would work.

She was on the verge of heading back to the estate when Ethan called her. When she explained what she was up to, he offered to act as her chauffeur.

"How was the wedding?" he asked as she slid into the passenger seat of his bright blue Mercedes twenty minutes later.

"It was beautiful. The ceremony was so heartfelt and romantic. I cried." She sighed at the memory. "Silly, isn't it? I don't even know Ryan and Zoe, but all I could think was how they belonged together."

A lump formed in Lia's throat as she recalled the way Ryan had looked at his bride. The love between them was like a stone tossed into a pond, rippling out from the couple to touch all the guests. She trembled as she recalled a moment during the vows when Paul's gaze had found hers amongst the well-wishers. The fleeting connection had sent a shock wave through Lia from head to toe.

"They really do," Ethan agreed. "It's as if everything that they went through created a one-of-a-kind connection between them."

Lia nodded. "That's what Paul said, as well."

"Paul said that?" Ethan blinked in surprise.

"I know, right?" She laughed. "It doesn't seem like him at all."

Ethan considered that for a moment. "I think his emotions go deeper than he lets on. He just needs someone he cares about to start breaking down his walls."

Lia didn't know how to respond, so she fidgeted with her phone. "While I was waiting for you to pick me up, I found a couple options at a dealer west of town."

"We can check those out, but I have a friend who owns a dealership and can get you a deal on something brand-new."

"I can't afford brand-new," Lia insisted.

"Paul and I discussed that and we'd like to help you out."

"That wasn't part of our original deal," she murmured ungraciously, as she revisited her mixed feelings about accepting the dress from the twins.

Obviously neither Paul nor Ethan understood that she didn't welcome the handout. While part of her acknowledged they perceived their offer as helpful, Lia resented being treated like a charity case.

"Well, we'd like to alter our original deal."

"Alter it how?"

"We were wondering if you could stick around another week."

For days she'd been bracing herself to leave on the date they'd agreed on. Lia contemplated Ethan's offer with a mixture of relief and dismay. As much as she wanted more time with Paul, this increased the risk that someone besides Dallas might suspect something was going on between them.

"Are you sure that's a good idea?" she asked. "Grady is doing so much better. I don't think there's any chance that his health will be impacted when he finds out I'm not Ava's daughter."

"I agree with you," Ethan said. "This was all Paul's idea."

Tears sprang to Lia's eyes, forcing her to turn her gaze to the passing landscape. She knew better than to read too much into what Ethan said. Paul might only be thinking of his grandfather's welfare and not have more personal motives.

"Is something wrong?"

She grasped for some explanation that would convince Ethan of the folly of her staying longer and recalled her conversation with Dallas the night before. Given how tight the twins were, how long could they count on Dallas to keep their secret?

"Something happened last night," she said.

"You don't say."

His tone was so sly that Lia blinked her eyes dry and turned to look at him. Something about his knowing grin sent a spike of anxiety straight through her.

Did he know? She and Paul were playing a dangerous game.

"Dallas knows I'm not your cousin," she blurted out, hoping to distract him.

"Oh."

"Just *oh*?" She'd braced herself to deal with his dismay. "Why aren't you more upset?"

"I guess that means the jig is up."

"Not yet," Lia replied, her frustration rising at his casual manner. Living in fear of being found out for nearly two weeks had taken a toll on her nerves. "I talked her out of telling anyone by promising it would only be a few more days before we tell Grady. So you see why we can't keep going with this."

"I'll talk to her," Ethan said. "Maybe if I explain and let her tell Poppy we can go a little longer."

"What if I don't want to stay?" Lia murmured.

"Is this because Paul didn't ask you himself?"

"Don't be ridiculous." But even as she denied it, heat surged into Lia's cheeks.

"I knew it," Ethan said, looking concerned. "I knew something was going on between you two."

"It's not like that." Even as she spoke, Lia could see that protesting was a waste of breath.

"It's exactly like that. Paul is attracted to you. And it looks as if his feelings are reciprocated."

"Well, yes. But it's just…" She'd almost said *sex.* "It's nothing serious."

"Are you sure?"

Lia fidgeted with her phone. "We're not in the least compatible."

"Here's where you're making assumptions. Has it occurred to you that he doesn't need someone who's like him, but someone who balances him? Someone who's lively and impulsive and knows exactly how to get him out of his head?"

The picture Ethan painted was tempting. Being the yin to Paul's yang appealed to Lia in every way. And it worked in the confines of their secret relationship. Taking things public would bring a whole new series of challenges.

"It might be good for him short-term," she said. "But in the end what he needs is a serious girlfriend. Someone who matches his ambition and his background. Someone he can be proud of."

"You don't think he can be proud of you?" Ethan asked, sounding surprised.

"Look at me." Lia gestured at her denim shorts and graphic T-shirt with its yoga-inspired pun. "I don't bring anything to the table."

"You shouldn't underestimate yourself," Ethan said. "I think you are one of the kindest, most delightful people I've ever met."

Lia forced a laugh. "Paul would say eccentric, impractical and frivolous."

"Maybe that's exactly what he needs."

"It would never work between us long-term," Lia said, musing that in her own way, she was as skittish about emotional entanglements as Paul.

Where he closed himself down and focused on work, she flitted from town to town, never really investing herself in any significant relationships. She was a butterfly. He was a rock. They couldn't possibly work.

"You matter to him," Ethan argued. "I just don't think he's figured out what to do about the way he's feeling. Give him time to adjust. He's never fallen in love before."

Ethan's words electrified Lia, stopping her heart. She pressed her shaking hands between her thighs, terrified that if she bought into Ethan's claim that she would only end up getting hurt. Yet even as she forced herself to be practical, her heart clamored for her to stay in Charleston and be with Paul. Be with him for how long?

"Do you know if he's still investigating me?" she asked, noting that the question surprised Ethan.

"He hasn't said anything. Why do you ask?"

As fast as she was falling for Paul, she needed to know if what was in her past would cause Paul to reject her.

"Paul has made it perfectly clear that he thinks I agreed to pretend to be your cousin because I'm up to no good."

"I'm pretty sure he's changed his mind on that score."

"Maybe." In fact, Lia wanted that to be true because

she hated to think that his doubts shadowed the moments she'd spent in his arms. "But I'm afraid he might discover something about me that he won't like."

Ethan frowned. "What sort of something?"

Lia gathered a bracing breath and began to explain about the man who'd swindled people out of hundreds of millions of dollars. Peter Thompson.

Her grandfather.

Ten

When Paul entered Grady's spacious living room prior to the family dinner, he discovered he was the last to arrive. In a matter of seconds he noted the placement of all his relatives throughout the room and had taken two steps toward Lia, following the instinct to be close to her, when his mother intercepted him.

"How was Ryan and Zoe's wedding?" Constance asked, seeming oblivious to the fact that she'd just stopped him from a huge blunder.

"Very nice."

"I never thought she and Tristan Crosby were well matched," his mother continued. "She seems much happier with Ryan."

"They're both happy," Paul declared.

"I don't suppose I'll be helping to plan any weddings

in the near future," Constance muttered, casting meaningful glances from Paul to Ethan.

"Isn't wedding planning usually left up to the bride and her family?" he countered, skillfully turning the conversation to less fraught waters. "You wouldn't want to step on anyone's toes."

"When have I ever overstepped?" Constance asked with studied innocence.

"Never."

But the truth was, Paul's mother was known for getting her way with the various charity events she helped organize. Was it any wonder both her sons had such strong leadership skills? They'd learned how to be in charge from a master.

Dinner was announced before Paul had a chance to do more than wave at his cousins and offer a smile to his aunt and uncle. Paul found himself seated between his father and Dallas, relegated to the opposite side of the table from Lia.

As always, Grady sat at the head. Tonight he was flanked by Lia and Lenora. Grady was in high spirits. Although he still struggled to speak, his eyes twinkled as he observed his family's interaction. The stark contrast in his vitality two weeks earlier lent an even greater festivity to the meal.

From his family's effusive remarks, Paul gathered the food was delicious, but he noticed little of what he tasted. He was preoccupied with Lia and pretending to maintain his interest in the twins' chatter or his father's concern about the imbalance in imports and exports due to the recent tariffs.

As dessert was served, Grady clinked his glass to gain everyone's attention. With each day, he gained more control over his words, but sometimes still relied on singing to produce certain sounds. Having gained everyone's attention, he began in a singsong rhythm.

Reaching for Lia's hand, Grady fixed his gaze on her. "I changed my will to include Lia."

Suspicion ran like poison through Paul's veins while Lia sat in stunned silence, wide eyes glued to Grady's face. Around the table, there were exclamations of approval. Paul locked gazes with his brother and saw his own concern mirrored there.

"This is quite sudden," Constance murmured with a slight frown. "I mean…" She seemed at a loss as she glanced from one son to the other.

Paul shook his head in an effort to communicate that this wasn't the moment to come clean. If they explained about the testing mistake on the heels of Grady's bombshell announcement, everyone would want to know why the delay in bringing up the issue. They couldn't afford any of the family asking questions that would clue Grady in to their scheme.

"You shouldn't have done that," Lia said, shaking her head. Her dismay seemed genuine. "It's… I don't…"

Her gaze darted Paul's way and just as quickly fled, leaving him unsure that she'd manipulated Grady into changing his will.

"You don't know me," she argued, her panic visibly threatening to choke her.

Grady shook his head, squeezed her hand and gave her a lopsided, reassuring smile. "You're my granddaughter," he announced in definitive tones, suggesting what was done was done.

As everyone finished off the red velvet cake, it was pretty obvious that Grady was fading. Although no one summoned her, Rosie appeared and wheeled him out of the room. Lia followed, but before she could escape upstairs, Paul drew her through the living room and out onto the side terrace.

Lia looked shell-shocked and near tears as she scanned his expression with near-frantic eyes. Paul balled his hands into fists to stop himself from taking her into his arms and soothing away her distress. He had so much to say, but didn't know where to start.

"This is a huge mess," Paul declared, his gut tight with conflicting emotion.

Before Lia could respond, Ethan appeared on the terrace. Her gaze went straight to him and clung like he was her lifeline.

"I had no idea he intended to change his will." Lia's voice was filled with anguish.

"You're sure he didn't mention it at all?" Paul demanded. "Because with a little warning we could've headed off his decision and saved us all a lot of grief."

Seeing her woeful expression, Ethan threw a protective arm around her shoulders and shot Paul a hard look that warned him to back off. "I'm sure if Lia knew she would've told us."

When Lia slumped against his brother's side, Paul felt like he'd been slapped.

"What are we going to do about this?" Irritation gave his voice a bite.

"Tell the truth," Lia said, sending a speaking glance Ethan's way. "The sooner the better."

But once they did Lia wouldn't have a reason to stay in Charleston any longer. He stared at Lia while the conversation at Ethan's house ran through his mind. The thought of her leaving made him ache.

"Let's give it a few days," Paul said. "If we explain about the testing service right now, the timing will look suspicious."

"I agree." Ethan nodded. "The damage is already done. A couple more days won't matter."

Lia grimaced. "I'm not sure that's true."

A significant look passed between Lia and Ethan, turning Paul into an unnecessary third wheel. What happened to the closeness he'd shared with Lia these last few days?

"Am I missing something?" Paul demanded.

"It's more complicated than you know," Lia admitted.

"More complicated how?"

"Why don't you and I grab a drink and I'll fill you in," Ethan said. Then, ignoring Paul's growing impatience, Ethan directed his next words to Lia. "I'll call you in the morning."

"Thank you."

Lia headed for the outside stairs that led to the second-floor terrace and was out of sight before Paul recovered from the bolt of jealousy that shot through him at the easy affection between Ethan and Lia. His resentment even overshadowed the shock of what their grandfather had done.

"What the hell?" Ethan demanded, as they left the house and crunched in the gravel side by side along the garden path on the way to their cars. "Why did you take your frustration out on Lia like that? None of this is her fault."

Paul grappled with dismay and self-loathing at the way he'd taken his shock and jealousy out on Lia. Although his first reaction to her being included in the will had been suspicion, he knew better. Instead he'd acted like she'd manipulated Grady, forcing Ethan to come to her defense.

But instead of owning his mistake, Paul lashed out. "I told you passing off a perfect stranger as Ava's daughter was going to blow up in our faces."

"Fine. You were right as always." Ethan's expression shifted into stubborn lines. "Look, fighting isn't going to do us any good. We need to figure out what to do."

"It's obvious we need to come clean to Grady immediately," Paul declared. "I'll tell him."

"We should both tell him," Ethan said. "It was my idea to let Grady believe she was his granddaughter. You should talk to Lia." Ethan's expression softened with pity. "Although after how you behaved just now, I'm not sure she's ever going to forgive you."

After leaving Paul and Ethan, Lia escaped to the solitude of her bedroom, intent on digesting the evening's events, and ran straight into more trouble. Dallas stood with her back to the windows, her arms crossed over her chest, wearing a scowl of open hostility. As soon as Lia closed the door for privacy, she rushed to reassure the younger woman.

"Please believe that I never meant for any of this to happen," Lia said, hating the way Dallas's eyes narrowed in suspicion. "I had no idea your grandfather was going to do that."

"This whole thing has gone too far," Dallas said, her voice an angry lash. "You need to tell everyone the truth."

"I agree," Lia assured her. "Ethan and Paul are talking about the best way to handle that right now."

"I really liked you." Dallas turned the declaration into an accusation. "I was so happy you were our cousin."

"The only family I ever had was my mother and since I turned eighteen and struck out on my own, I barely know where she is half the time." The sharp ache in Lia's chest made her next words almost impossible to get out. "You have no idea how much I wanted to be part of your family."

"But you're not." Some of Lia's anguish must have penetrated Dallas's outrage because her next words were gentler. "And that really sucks."

"I'm sorry I upset you, but I never meant for anyone to get hurt," Lia protested, overpowered by loss.

"You should've thought about that before you lied."

Dallas left the bedroom without another word and Lia threw herself facedown on the bed. For several minutes she wallowed in misery while her eyes burned with unshed tears. She'd deserved to be called out for her lies. Lia just wished it didn't hurt so much.

As Lia pondered her next course of action she realized it was time for her to leave Charleston. Earlier that day she'd purchased a truck. Not the fancy brand-new vehicle Ethan had insisted he and Paul wanted to buy for her, but one within her budget. After some determined negotiating, she emptied her savings account and left the lot the proud owner of a five-year-old model similar to the one that had been totaled six months earlier, but with fewer miles on it and a working air conditioner.

The purchase compelled her to confront what she'd been avoiding since the wedding. In the days before the romantic event, as she'd recognized her feelings for Paul were developing into love, she'd toyed with giving up her vagabond ways to be with him. Tonight she'd come to grips with reality. No matter how strong her attachment to Paul, his stark accusation demonstrated that without trust he couldn't love her with the openness and honesty she needed. Settling for anything less would lead to heartbreak.

Halfway through her packing, Lia noticed her duffel held more than when she'd arrived. The fact that she'd begun to collect unessential items revealed a shift in her attitude. There was nothing extravagant or indulgent in the miscellaneous clothes and accessories she'd let the twins encourage her to buy, but the purchases suited the life she'd been living in Charleston.

After stacking her costume boxes and overflowing duffel by the door, Lia crossed the hall and gently knocked on Grady's door. She owed him the truth and an apology before she left.

Later, she would call Ethan and say goodbye. Although she was angry with Ethan and herself for the ruse, he'd been a good friend to her. And he'd worry if she just vanished.

That left Paul. Her heart clenched in regret. Would he even care that she was leaving? She'd been a fool to imagine that she'd won him over, that his poor opinion of her had changed, could change. Instead, his suspicions had merely lain dormant, waiting for something terrible to happen.

No, she couldn't face him again. Couldn't confront the suspicion in his eyes and be devastated by his stubborn refusal to believe that she'd had no interest in financial gain. Now that she was leaving, Lia was overwhelmed with relief that she'd never face Paul's dismay about her grandfather.

When Grady called for her to enter, Lia stepped into the room and crossed to where he sat in bed. Setting aside the book he'd been reading, he smiled at her with such joy that a lump formed in her throat. She might not be his granddaughter, but she loved him and was ashamed that she'd ever lied to him.

At that moment, Lia knew that no matter what the brothers decided over drinks tonight, she had to speak the real truth. Not the story they'd concocted about the mistake with the DNA matching, but the fact that there'd never been a genetic test.

Dropping to her knees beside his bed, Lia touched his arm. "I want you to know that these last couple weeks have been some of the happiest of my life." Her voice faltered, but she cleared her throat and kept going. "You have made me feel welcome and nothing I can say or do could ever repay your kindness."

Grady frowned down at her, obviously perplexed. "What's wrong?"

She couldn't get over how much progress he'd made with his speech, and hated that she was leaving before she could help him make more.

"I'm so sorry." Lia closed her eyes to block out his face for this next part. "The thing is, I'm not your granddaughter."

Grady gripped her hand. "What?"

Lia's heart broke as she continued. "I feel terrible. It's all been a huge misunderstanding. The genetic testing…" She stumbled on her words, needing a moment to collect herself. "We made that up because you were so convinced that I was your granddaughter and you got better because of it. You'd been looking for Ava's daughter for so long, and we just wanted you to be happy. And then you changed your will. And now it's all just a big confusing mess." The words flowed out of her in a great rush. She didn't realize she was crying until Grady's knuckles brushed her cheek and she saw how they came away damp. "I know you must be so upset and I never meant to cause you pain."

She'd surveyed him as she spoke and saw that he was confused and shocked, but her confession hadn't devastated him. In fact, the way he kept patting her hand conveyed he was more concerned that she was so upset.

"We were going to tell you in a few days because you've been doing so much better. Before now we were afraid you'd stop trying to get well again. I know I shouldn't have gone along with it, but Ethan was so desperate and then Paul was forced to keep our secret because he didn't want to put your recovery at risk. It wasn't his fault. And please don't blame Ethan. Your family has been so warm and welcoming. But then you included me in your will and I'm not really your grand-daughter." Lia paused to get her ragged breathing under control and peered at Grady. "You are going to be okay, aren't you? Please tell me I haven't made things worse."

"I'm fine."

"Oh good." She squeezed his hand. "I'm glad be-cause I need to leave Charleston and I couldn't go if I thought you might relapse."

"No." Grady shook his head. "Stay."

"I can't. When your family find out I lied about being Ava's daughter, they will all hate me."

"Not everyone," Grady said. "Not me."

The sight of his earnest smile blurred as fresh tears formed in Lia's eyes. If the only opinion that mattered belonged to the patriarch of the Watts family, Lia knew she'd stay and work hard to earn everyone's trust. But she was really running from Paul's reaction, recogniz-ing that he could never trust her because of what lurked in her past.

"The thing is," she whispered, barely able to speak past the raw tightness in her throat. "There's also this issue with my grandfather being a thief and a liar. He's a terrible person and because we're related everyone will think I'm a terrible person, too. Even though I've never met him."

Lia paused to gulp in air, unable to believe she'd

blurted out the truth about her grandfather on top of all the other revelations.

"And since I'm confessing everything… I'm in love with Paul and he doesn't love me, so it's too painful for me to stay." Lia pushed to her feet and dropped a fleeting kiss on Grady's cheek. "I want you to know that being a part of your family was the best thing that ever happened to me."

Eleven

Paul barely slept and was on his third cup of coffee when his phone chimed, letting him know he'd received a text. His stomach muscles clenched in reaction. Had Lia finally replied to his messages from the previous night? Her lack of response from the first one had prompted him to send another apology late in the night, asking if they could talk. That she hadn't acknowledged that one either was eating him alive.

A hundred times since last night he'd pledged if she gave him another chance, he would never doubt her again. But as the hours ticked by, he grew less confident that she would give him a hearing.

Glancing at the screen, he discovered the text was from Dallas and not Lia. With the bleak landscape of his future stretched before him, he cued up his messaging app and read his cousin's text.

I did something terrible and now Lia's gone.

Before he could reach out to Dallas about her ominous message, a call from Ethan lit up his smartphone.

"I just talked to Lia," Ethan said, sounding grim.

"She called you?" The words tasted like sawdust. Could he blame her for choosing the brother who'd had her back the night before? "Is she okay? I just got a text from Dallas saying that Lia is gone. Did she say where?"

The night before, he and Ethan had discussed how to handle the revelation that Lia wasn't Ava's daughter and decided to stick to their original story about the testing service getting things wrong instead of telling Grady the truth. She'd been a reluctant coconspirator and shouldn't have to face Grady's anger.

"She's at her camper," Ethan said.

"What's she doing there?"

"I don't think she felt comfortable staying at the estate any longer," Ethan said. "She told Grady the whole story last night."

Paul cursed, remembering how she'd pushed for the truth to come out. "How did he take it? Is he okay?"

"She said he was shocked, but okay when she left. I'm heading over there now."

"Why did she do that?" Paul mused. "We had it handled."

"Maybe because she has more integrity than both of us put together."

Ethan's ironic tone recalled all the accusations Paul had lobbed at her. He knew his brother was right. While they'd all lied, Lia had been the only one who'd done so without selfish motives. She'd declared time and again that she only wanted to help. And that's what she'd done.

Whereas he'd been inspired to sacrifice his own integrity by the desperate need to keep his grandfather alive and the return of Grady's approval. When had guilt stopped eating at him? Somewhere around the first time he'd kissed Lia. After that, he'd been less conflicted about lying to his grandfather and more disturbed by how she affected him.

"Here's the other thing," Ethan continued. "The reason she's at her camper is because she's preparing to leave Charleston."

"Leave?" Paul's chest tightened, robbing him of breath. "When?"

Ethan's tone was hoarse with sympathy as he answered. "She might already be gone."

Blind panic rose at the thought, and after arranging to meet Ethan at the estate in an hour, Paul hung up on his brother. With clumsy fingers he immediately dialed Lia's number, praying that this time she'd answer.

"Ethan says you're leaving," he declared the instant she engaged the call.

"Yes." She sounded shaken, but determined. "I have to."

"No, you don't."

"Grady knows I'm not Ava's daughter."

"I'll make him understand that none of this was your fault."

"But it was my fault. I never should've pretended to be something I'm not." The catch in her voice tore at Paul's heart. "It'll be better once I'm gone. Your family can put it behind you," she finished.

"Don't worry about my family," he said, feeling ragged and unsteady. "Ethan and I will sort everything out. Please don't go. I know Grady won't want you to leave town. He loves you."

Even as he spoke the words, Paul winced. Why hadn't he told her how miserable he would be if she left? Using Grady as an excuse was cowardly.

"Not me. He loves his granddaughter." Her bleak tones told him any attempt to convince her was wasted breath. "I'm really sorry if I created trouble for you and Ethan by telling Grady the truth," Lia said, a somber warble in her voice.

"Don't worry about Ethan and me. We can take a punch." He stripped all humor out of his voice before saying, "I'm heading to the estate now. Afterward I think you and I need to talk."

"There's nothing more to say."

Oh, there was plenty to say. It just depended on whether he had the guts to declare how he felt about her. "Please don't leave Charleston."

"I have to go," she declared, her urgent need to run coming through loud and clear. "Don't you understand?"

Paul shook his head. He did, but that didn't mean he'd stop trying to persuade her to stay. "Promise me you won't leave town without seeing me first."

"I'll only promise I won't leave today."

That didn't leave him much time. "I'll come by after I see Grady. Where can I find you?"

"I'll be at my camper."

Disconnecting the call with things so unresolved between them was one of the hardest things Paul had ever done, but he trusted her when she promised to stick around until he could get there.

When he arrived at the estate, Paul met his brother near the pool and together they found their grandfather in the library on the first floor. The room was at the back of the house with dual access to the outside terraces. White bookshelves, trim and wainscoting offset the red walls, giving the room a lived-in, cozy feel. Little had changed since his grandmother's death nearly fifty years earlier except for the addition of children's books and thrillers beside the classic novels Delilah Watts had loved.

As soon as they entered the room, Grady spoke. "You lied to me."

"It was all my idea," Ethan explained. "Don't be mad at Paul or Lia. We just wanted you to get better, and from the moment you believed that Lia was your granddaughter, you did."

"It wasn't just Ethan," Paul chimed in, refusing to let his brother shoulder the full blame. "I went along with the ruse, as well. We really did believe it was for your own good."

Grady scowled. "I changed my will."

"We didn't expect that," Ethan admitted, speaking before Paul could. "Our plan had been to tell you this week that the testing service had made a mistake."

"But then you put Lia in your will and everything blew up," Paul added.

"And just so you know, none of this was her idea," Ethan said. "I tricked her that day at the hospital."

"She only went along with it because she wanted to help you." Awash in misery, Paul willed his grandfather to believe that Lia was genuine. "That's all she's ever done."

"I know," Grady said, his words coming with slow, deliberate care. "I don't blame her."

"Does she know that?" Paul asked. "Because she's leaving town. Running away from Charleston. From us." *From me.*

"I told her." Grady shook his head. "She's afraid."

"Of what?"

"Of you."

Paul recoiled from Grady's censure. "I'd never do anything to hurt her."

"Last night—" Ethan began.

"I screwed up." Paul interrupted, glaring at his brother. "And then I made it worse because I got mad when you jumped to her rescue." His irritation faded as he realized how stupid his defense sounded. "I'm an idiot for not believing in her. And she's leaving town because of it." Paul dropped into a chair and let his head fall into his hands. "How do I convince her to stay?"

"Have you told her you're in love with her?" Ethan asked in exasperated tones. "From what I've heard women really go for that."

"I'm not..." he began instinctively, shocked at his brother's revelation. Paul glanced from him to Grady and saw curiosity rather than surprise on his grandfather's lean face.

"Not what?" Ethan demanded. "Not in love? Not sure she'd trust you with her heart? I don't know that I'd blame her."

Paul struggled to wrap his head around what truth lay in his heart. Is this what love felt like? An obsessive hunger to be around her all the time? To revel in blazing joy and suffer terrifying despair in the space of minutes?

And while Lia's generous spirit and upbeat sincerity had gotten beneath his skin, Paul didn't know how to surrender to a relationship that challenged his black-and-white views. Lia's belief in all things metaphysical, her flighty, impulsive need to live a nomadic existence, her lack of substantial ties to people and place ran contrary to what was important to him.

"You're right," Paul said, aching at the thought that she intended to leave him. What could he say or do to convince her to give up her nomadic ways and stay in one place? With him. "I love her, but I messed up big time. She won't stay for me."

Grady shook his head. "She loves you."

For a second Paul couldn't breathe. He shifted his gaze from his grandfather's fond smile to Ethan's exasperated expression. Hope rose.

"Are you sure?" The level of desperation in his voice shook him.

"She's been falling in love with you from the first," his brother said. "I have no idea why. You've been a complete jerk."

"The whole time," Paul agreed, unable to imagine how she'd managed to see something of value in him.

When he wasn't pummeling her with distrust, he'd been battling the unsettling emotions that turned him inside out. He wasn't the least bit lovable. And then he realized the familiar path down which his thoughts had taken him. Damn it. He was still questioning her judgment. Maybe the time had come for him to accept that he had much to learn from her.

"How do I fix this?" he asked the room at large.

"You could start by telling her that you can't live without her," his brother said. "And that you have her back. Then remind her that we all love her and everyone believes she only had Grady's best interests at heart."

"What if I can't convince her?"

Ethan ejected a curse. "When did you become the guy who gives up? Is that what you do when your clients have a data breech?"

"No."

"So why with something that is so much more important than all the hackers you chase put together are you just quitting?"

The question, combined with Grady's disgusted expression, caused Paul's gut to twist in shame. He hated that Ethan was right. Was he really going to let her go? Without a fight? What was wrong with him?

All at once everything became so clear to him. He loved her. She loved him. He just needed to figure out a way to convince her they were meant for each other. In a flash he knew exactly what it would take to convince Lia that he was the man for her. The brilliance of it made him grin.

"I have to go."

"Wait." The single word came from Grady. He pulled something out of his pocket and held it out to Paul. "Give this to Lia."

Feeling slightly light-headed, Paul opened the small box and saw a familiar diamond ring tucked into the black velvet. "This is Grandma's ring," he murmured in awe.

Grady's lopsided smile bloomed as he nodded. "Make her my granddaughter."

Clutching the small box, Paul left the library and raced downstairs.

The trip from the estate to where Lia was keeping her camper felt as if it took forever, but it was only a forty-minute drive. He took advantage of the time to rehearse what he intended to say to her. He started with *I love you* and ended with *Will you spend the rest of your life with me?* What came in between would be all the reasons why she made his life better. Her laugh. Her giving nature. Her sweetness. Her free-spirited ways. Her beauty.

He didn't deserve her. But from now on, he'd work damn hard to.

When he reached the spot where her camper had last been parked, he saw it was gone. He gripped the steering wheel in dismay, unable to believe she'd leave after promising to wait for him. Several seconds ticked by while he brought his doubts back under control.

Lia hadn't left. She'd given her word and she was the type of woman who kept her promises. He turned around and headed toward the shop to find out where the camper had been moved to. To his relief, as he rounded the final corner, he spied it near the water station. She was filling the tanks with water in preparation for starting out.

He parked his SUV so that it blocked her truck and hopped out. Finding himself oddly out of breath, he strode toward her. There was wariness, not welcome, in her hazel eyes as he stopped before her.

"You can't leave," he began, suddenly awkward. Incapacitated by growing panic, he stood looking at her with a pounding heart.

"You have to be kidding," she said, shutting off the water and replacing the hose. "Now that this whole ridiculous scheme is over and everyone knows I'm not Ava's daughter, no one will want me to stay."

"I do." He came over and took her hands in his. "Stay in Charleston with me."

She shook her head and wouldn't meet his gaze. "Why?"

"Because I love you."

Her conversation with Ethan hadn't prepared her for Paul's actual declaration. His open and earnest manner as much as the words he spoke stunned her. Paul loved her. Her heart sang with joy. For days she'd been arguing with herself, seeking ways to make her relationship with Paul work.

If she was too quirky for Charleston society, she

could dress differently and learn to discuss what was important to Paul's friends. Giving up the road wouldn't be a hardship if it meant waking up every morning beside the sexy cybersecurity specialist. Already he'd had a grounding influence on her. She'd even imagined herself going to school and becoming an occupational therapist, helping others the way she had Grady.

But then she remembered all that stood between them. She'd deceived his family. Her grandfather had swindled investors out of millions. Their vastly different natures. Any one of those things would create challenges. All three together were insurmountable.

"I don't know…"

"You don't know?" Paul's outrage clearly indicated he was under the misguided assumption that all he had to do was declare himself and she'd fall at his feet in gratitude. Lia's annoyance gave her the fortitude to resist the romantic longing building in her.

"Ethan said that you've never been in love before," she explained, determined to do the smart thing. "And that you're conflicted."

"Maybe I was before. But that's not how I feel anymore."

"And tomorrow?" she persisted. "When something comes up about my past that triggers your suspicions again?"

He frowned. "What's going to come up?"

"I don't know." She waved her hands around. "My mother could show up and shock you with her passion for taking nude photos of herself. Or you could judge me because I have no idea who my father is." She sucked in a shaky breath and braced herself for his reaction. "Or maybe the fact that my grandfather is Peter Thompson."

His obvious shock at the familiar name confirmed what he'd thought about her all along and sparked her greatest fear. He'd always perceived her as the fruit of a poisonous tree. Still, she couldn't deny a certain amount of relief at getting everything out in the open.

"That's right," she continued. "I'm the granddaughter of one of the country's most notorious swindlers. His Ponzi scheme defrauded investors of hundreds of millions of dollars. The scandal rocked Seattle and devastated my family. It's why my mother changed her name and lives off the grid. It's why I do what I can to help people. I'm related to a liar and a thief who harmed thousands. You were right about me all along."

Paul captured her hands and squeezed gently. "I wasn't right about you at all. That was the problem. I judged you before I knew what a kind, loving, selfless person you are."

"My grandfather is a criminal," Lia said, compelled to point out the obvious.

"A fact that has nothing to do with who you are."

As tempting as it was to accept his breezy dismissal of her background, Lia couldn't believe he'd just let it go. "But it's a scandal that could come to light. I can't imagine your family will appreciate that."

"If it does, we'll deal with it," Paul declared. "You are exactly what I need in my life. Someone to remind me to laugh and to stop working and to enjoy myself. You've made me feel again. Or for the first time. And now that you've opened me up, I need you so I will stay this way."

"But you said it yourself, we're completely different. How long before I start to drive you crazy?"

"Immediately." He laughed and his happiness made her heart pound. "Don't you get it? I'm thrilled that you do. Isn't that what your tarot cards said? For too long I've been burying myself in work. Isolating myself from the people I love and the world at large. You brought me back from the wilderness."

She couldn't believe he remembered the reading much less had taken it so to heart. "Does that mean you believe a little?"

"I'm starting to believe a lot. And that's all because of you."

"But what if I don't want to settle down in one place?"

"I can do my job from wherever," he said. "If you get itchy feet, we'll load up your little camper and take it on the road. Have laptop will travel," he joked, but to Lia's surprise and delight, it looked as if he meant it.

Still, if he'd taught her anything these last few weeks it was caution. "It sounds like a fairy-tale ending," she said. "But I'm not a princess, I just play one for kids who are stuck in the hospital."

"I have an idea." He turned utterly serious. "You read tarot cards for me and my cousins, but you never did one for yourself."

"I don't generally do my own readings."

"Because you can't?"

"Because I don't want to see what's coming."

"How about for just this once, you take a look. If the cards tell you to get back on the road without me, then you'll know."

She laughed, unable to believe what she was hearing. Paul Watts was going to let his future be shaped by something he claimed not to believe in? "If you truly wanted me to stay, I would think you'd be trying to convince me yourself instead of depending on the cards."

"I haven't stopped trying to convince you. And I think the tarot cards will show you that you belong here. With me. Come on. It'll be fun."

Lia wanted to argue, but the obstinate set of Paul's jaw kept her silent.

"Fine," she said, heading toward the camper. "Let's do this."

In the hours since she'd said goodbye to Grady, she'd restored Misty to her preferred organized state. As she pulled out the tarot deck and sat down at the snug dinette, she noticed the way Paul glanced around, his gaze lingering on the bed where they'd made love the first time. Her heart skipped as stony determination settled over his features. That this man wanted her, loved her, weakened Lia's resolve to make a clearheaded decision. She'd followed her intuition all her life, impulsively jumping into action, but some of Paul's deliberate, logic-driven methodology had rubbed off on her.

Beneath Paul's intense regard, Lia shuffled the cards while asking a simple question. Should she stay in Charleston and be with Paul? Instead of laying out the Celtic Cross spread all at once with the cards face-down the way she'd done in the earlier readings, Lia slowly placed each card faceup, considering the meaning as she went.

The reading started out ordinarily enough with the Fool, signifying the beginning of a journey, covered by the Two of Swords, which had a picture of a blindfolded woman, with arms crossed over her chest, holding two swords. The defensive imagery was clear enough that even Paul blinked in startled understanding.

"The basis of the situation is the Four of Cups," she narrated. "Indicating a situation where someone is apathetic about the same dull situation."

"Meaning it's time for you to leave Charleston?"

Or that she wasn't as enthusiastic to get back on the road as she once might have been. In truth, as she'd prepared the camper to leave, she'd noticed a dullness in her movements, a depression at the idea of leaving behind a city she'd grown to love.

"Possibly," she answered, laying down the card symbolizing the recent past. "The Lovers." Since that interpretation was also incredibly obvious, she moved on to possible outcome. "Eight of Cups." The card showed a man walking away from what had been a happy situation. Lia's heart sank as the message began to materialize.

"The King of Swords," Paul said when he saw the next card. "Is that me in your future?"

Obviously, he'd been paying attention during the readings she'd done for his cousins because there'd been all sorts of kings in their spreads that Lia had interpreted as the significant appearance of strong men in the lives.

"I believe so," Lia said cautiously. In the self position

she drew the Six of Swords. It showed a couple traveling across the water in a boat, indicating a journey. The fact that it was reversed suggested the travel would be unsatisfying. "In my environment," she continued, placing another from the sword suit.

"That doesn't look good," Paul remarked, gazing at the Nine of Swords which depicted a woman crying against a backdrop of swords. "In fact, she looks pretty unhappy. Seems like your leaving is going to upset people."

Refusing to give him the satisfaction of agreeing, Lia placed the next card. "Hopes and fears." Her reaction to the card's significance must have shown on her face because Paul eyed her intently.

"What does it mean?"

Lia ground her teeth and debated whether to share that the card indicated the end of a journey or explain the more commonly held understanding that the Eight of Wands quite literally read as arrows of love.

"Action taken in love affairs," she grumbled. "Proposals made and accepted."

Although Lia didn't glance at Paul, she could feel the smugness radiating from him.

"And the outcome card?"

She froze, afraid to see what her future held. So much of the reading confirmed Paul's belief that she needed to stay and give their relationship a chance. How many times had she told people to trust in what the universe was telling them through the tarot deck? To turn her back on such clear mystic advice meant denying what she believed in.

And why?

Because she was afraid to take a risk with Paul.

"Lia?" Paul's gentle prompt brought a lump to her throat. "What's the last card?"

"I'm afraid to find out," she admitted. "In this moment, right here and now, I haven't made a decision that will impact the rest of my life. I'm at a crossroads where I can see my life going either way and there's a certain amount of peace in that."

"Schrödinger's cat," he declared, in all his adorable nerdiness. "Until you see the outcome you are both staying in Charleston and taking a chance on us while also content to drive off and never look back." Paul plucked the last card from the top of the deck and placed it facedown in its position. "Forget the cards and trust your heart."

That heart was hammering so hard against her ribs that Lia could barely breathe. Loving him consumed her, but she couldn't shake the anxiety that one day he'd wake up and regret asking her to stay.

"It's not my heart I need to trust," she told him, pointing to the King of Swords card that represented him in the near-future position. "You rule your world with the strength of your personality and intellect."

Paul indicated the card that represented her. The Fool. A free spirit. Impulsive. Naive. Trusting that a leap of faith will bring joy and happiness.

"It's why I need someone like you in my life. We've known each other two weeks and I've changed so much in that short period of time. If you leave, I'll just go back to being lonely and isolated, only now that state will make me miserable." He then pointed to the Eight of Cups in her potential outcome position. "Don't leave behind what promises to be a wonderful life with me here."

"But your family," she protested. "I lied to all of them about being Ava's daughter. How can I ever look them in the eye again?"

"Actually, several of them already knew," Paul said. "Ethan told Dad and we suspect he told Mom."

"Dallas confronted me last night and she was really upset that Grady wrote me into his will," Lia admitted, hope fading even as she noted the gentleness that softened the strong lines of Paul's handsome face. "I think she hates me."

"She doesn't. She texted me this morning after she realized you left and knows she handled things badly. My whole family loves you. And I love you. The only question that remains is whether you love us enough to become a permanent member of the Watts clan."

Her breath stopped. "What do you mean by permanent?"

"I mean…" He grinned at her as he slid out of the dinette. Dropping to one knee beside her, Paul popped open the ring box Grady had given him. "Ophelia Marsh, will you do me the honor of becoming my wife?"

The formal words filled her with joy. "I adore you, Paul Watts," she murmured around the thick lump in her throat. "But…" Panic rose; she wanted so badly to belong that she could barely keep it together. "Your family has to approve."

"This is my grandmother's ring," he told her, pulling

the circle of white gold and glittering diamonds free of the velvet padding. "Grady gave it to me to give to you. He wants you to be a part of our family. We all do."

Lia stared at the ring, the legacy of an earlier generation's love and fidelity, and something shifted inside her, settling into place, making her whole for the first time in her life. She held out her left hand and let Paul slide the ring onto her finger.

She framed his face with her hands and smiled. "Nothing would make me happier than to spend the rest of my life with you."

As Paul leaned forward to kiss her, he reached out and turned over the outcome card. Lia caught a glimpse of the image an instant before his lips met hers.

The Sun.

Joy. Happiness. Optimism. Energy. Wonder. The card promised all these and more.

Brilliant light exploded behind her closed eyelids as she gloried in the perfection of his kiss and reveled in all the boundless possibilities the future held. As opposites they'd been attracted to each other. Through their differences they'd learned, struggled and eventually changed. Like yin and yang they belonged together, two halves that made up a whole. Their journey had been a blend of destiny and deliberate choices. And as many challenges as they might encounter in the years ahead, Lia trusted they would overcome them together.

Epilogue

In the midst of the party to celebrate their engagement, Paul took Lia's hand and drew her away from the well-wishers. Since arriving at his grandfather's estate, they'd been swarmed by family and friends all eager to congratulate them. It was their first major social event as a couple and he'd been worried how she'd handle all the attention, but her dazzling smile demonstrated that she was gaining confidence by the hour.

Much had happened in the weeks since he'd proposed. Grateful for all she'd done for him, Grady had left Lia in his will, but since she wasn't Ava's daughter, he'd changed the amount intended for her. On the matter of Lia's background, they'd chosen to reveal her family connection to the infamous Peter Thompson. By controlling the way the story came out, they'd gotten ahead of the gossip. Still, when faced with so much unwanted media attention, Paul half expected Lia to bolt for the open road. Instead, supported by the entire Watts family, she'd weathered the news event with grace.

Craving a few minutes alone with Lia, Paul guided her onto the back terrace and into a dark corner away from prying eyes. He didn't expect they'd have more than a few minutes alone before they were discovered. He desperately needed to kiss her. As if her own desires matched his, Lia melted into his embrace, sliding her fingers into his hair and applying pressure to coax his lips to hers.

The scent of her perfume reminded him of the first time they'd met. He realized now that he'd started falling for her in that moment. His tactics for scaring her off would've worked if Ethan hadn't concocted his scheme to pass her off as Grady's granddaughter. Realizing just how close he'd come to losing her made Paul tighten his arms around Lia's slim waist.

"I thought we were done sneaking around," she teased with a breathless laugh when they finally came up for air.

"With a family as large as mine, if we want privacy we're going to have to get creative."

She hummed with pleasure as his lips traveled down her neck. "I like getting creative with you."

The sound of a door opening a short distance away made Paul groan. A second later he heard Ethan's voice.

"Here's where you two disappeared off to."

"Go away," Paul growled, not ready for his interlude with Lia to end. "We're busy."

Ethan ignored his brother's attempts to send him packing and stepped closer. "I thought you both might be interested in learning that we've received a hit from the testing service."

Paul's breath caught as the momentous news hit him like a sharp jab to his gut. Lia clutched his arm as she, too, reacted. Their eyes met and in that moment of connection the rest of the world fell away. Paul reveled in the deep bond developing between them. No matter what happened in the future, Paul knew Lia would be beside him, offering support and performing the occasional tarot card reading.

He grinned down at her. "I love you."

"I love you, too," Lia echoed, her sweet smile setting his heart on fire.

"Did you two hear what I said?" Ethan demanded, his exasperation coming through loud and clear. "We found Ava's daughter."

* * * * *

*Don't miss a single installment of
Sweet Tea and Scandal:*

Upstairs Downstairs Baby
Substitute Seduction
Revenge with Benefits
Seductive Secrets

*by Cat Schield,
available exclusively
from Harlequin Desire.*

Get 4 FREE REWARDS!

We'll send you 2 FREE Books plus 2 FREE Mystery Gifts.

Harlequin® Desire books feature heroes who have it all: wealth, status, incredible good looks... everything but the right woman.

FREE
Value Over
$20

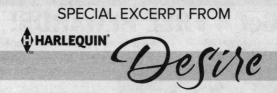
"I'll tell you what," he said. "I'm going to give you a kiss.
And if afterward you can walk away, then you should."

She blinked. "I don't want to."

"See how you feel after the kiss."

He dropped the ax, and it hit the frozen ground with a
dull thump.

He already knew.

He already knew that he was going to have a hard time
getting his hands off her once they'd been on her. The
way that she appealed to him hit a primitive part of him
he couldn't explain. A part of him that was something
other than civilized.

She took a step toward him, those ridiculous high
heels somehow skimming over the top of the dirt and
rocks. She was soft and elegant, and he was half-dressed

and sweaty from chopping wood, his breath a cloud in the cold air.

She reached out and put her hand on his chest. And it took every last ounce of his willpower not to grab her wrist and pin her palm to him. To hold her against him, make her feel the way his heart was beginning to rage out of control.

He couldn't remember the last time he'd wanted a woman like this.

And he didn't know if it was the touch of the forbidden adding to the thrill, or if it was the fact that she wanted his body and nothing else. Because he could do nothing for Emerson Maxfield, not Holden Brown, the man he was pretending to be. The man who had to depend on the good graces of his employer and lived in a cabin on the property. There was nothing he could do for her.

She didn't even want emotions from him.

But this woman standing in front of him truly wanted only this elemental thing, this spark of heat between them to become a blaze.

And who was he to deny her?

*Will their first kiss lead to something more
than either expected?*

Find out in
Rancher's Wild Secret
by New York Times *bestselling author Maisey Yates.*

*Available November 2019 wherever
Harlequin® Desire books and ebooks are sold.*

Harlequin.com

Want to give in to temptation with
steamy tales of irresistible desire?

Check out **Harlequin® Presents®,
Harlequin® Desire** and
Harlequin® Kimani™ Romance books!

New books available every month!

CONNECT WITH US AT:

Facebook.com/groups/HarlequinConnection

 Facebook.com/HarlequinBooks

Twitter.com/HarlequinBooks

 Instagram.com/HarlequinBooks

 Pinterest.com/HarlequinBooks

ReaderService.com

HHARLEQUIN®

**ROMANCE WHEN
YOU NEED IT**

PGENRE2018

Love Harlequin romance?

DISCOVER.

Be the first to find out about promotions, news and exclusive content!

 Facebook.com/HarlequinBooks

Twitter.com/HarlequinBooks

 Instagram.com/HarlequinBooks

Pinterest.com/HarlequinBooks

ReaderService.com

EXPLORE.

Sign up for the Harlequin e-newsletter and download a free book from any series at **TryHarlequin.com.**

CONNECT.

Join our Harlequin community to share your thoughts and connect with other romance readers!
Facebook.com/groups/HarlequinConnection

**ROMANCE WHEN
YOU NEED IT**

HSOCIAL2018

THE WORLD IS BETTER WITH

Romance

Harlequin has everything from contemporary, passionate and heartwarming to suspenseful and inspirational stories.

Whatever your mood,
we have a romance just for you!

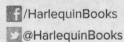